Meg Cabot has lived in Indiana and California, USA, and in France. She has worked as an assistant dorm manager of a large university, an illustrator, and a writer of historical romance (under a different name). She currently lives in New York City with her husband and a one-eyed cat called Henrietta, and says she is still waiting for her real parents, the king and queen, to come and restore her to her rightful throne.

Visit Meg Cabot's website at www.megcabot.com

D1548785

The PRINCESS DIARIES

Third Time Lucky

Meg Cabot

MACMILLAN CHILDREN'S BOOKS

First published 2001 by HarperCollins Children's Books, USA
a division of HarperCollins*Publishers*

This edition published 2002 by Macmillan Children's Books

a division of Macmillan Publishers Limited
20 New Wharf Road, London N1 9RR
Basingstoke and Oxford
www.panmacmillan.com

Associated companies throughout the world

ISBN 0 330 48207 6

17 19 18 16

A CIP catalogue record for this book is available from
the British Library.

Typeset by Intype London Ltd
Printed and bound in Great Britain by
Mackays of Chatham plc, Chatham, Kent

Many thanks to Beth Ader, Jennifer Brown, Barbara Cabot, Sarah Davies, Alison Donalty, Laura Langlie, Abby McAden, David Walton, and especially Benjamin Egnatz.

'One of Sara's "pretends" is that she is a princess. She plays it all the time – even in school. She wants Ermengarde to be one too, but Ermengarde says she is too fat.'

'She *is* too fat,' said Lavinia. 'And Sara is too thin.'

'Sara says it has nothing to do with what you look like, or what you have. It has only to do with what you *think* of, and what you *do*.'

A Little Princess
Frances Hodgson Burnett

English Class

Assignment (Due December 8)

Here at Albert Einstein High School we have a very diverse student population. Over one hundred and seventy different nations, religions and ethnic groups are represented by our student body. In the space below, describe the manner in which your family celebrates the uniquely American holiday, Thanksgiving. Please utilize appropriate margins.

My Thanksgiving
by Mia Thermopolis

6:45 a.m.
Roused by the sound of my mother vomiting. She is well into her third month of pregnancy now. According to her obstetrician, all the throwing up should stop in the next trimester. I can't wait. I have been marking the days off on my *N Sync calendar. (I don't really like *N Sync. At least, not that much. My best friend Lilly bought me the calendar as a joke. Except that one guy really is pretty cute.)

7:45 a.m.
Mr Gianini, my new stepfather, knocks on my door. Only now I am supposed to call him Frank. This is very difficult to remember due to the fact that at school, where he is my second period Algebra teacher, I am supposed to call him Mr Gianini. So I just don't call him anything (to his face).

   It's time to get up, Mr Gianini says. We are having Thanksgiving at his parents' house on Long Island. We have to leave now if we are going to beat the traffic.

There is no traffic this early on Thanksgiving Day. We arrive at Mr G's parents' house in Sagaponack three hours early.

Mrs Gianini (Mr Gianini's mother, not my mother. My mother is still Helen Thermopolis because she is fairly well-known as a painter under that name, and also because she does not believe in the cult of the patriarchy) is still in curlers. She looks very surprised. This might not only be because we arrived so early, but also because no sooner had my mother entered the house than she was forced to run for the bathroom with her hand pressed over her mouth, on account of the smell of the roasting turkey. I am hoping this means that my future half-brother or sister is a vegetarian, since the smell of meat cooking used to make my mother hungry, not nauseated.

My mother already informed me in the car on the way over from Manhattan that Mr Gianini's parents are very old-fashioned and are used to enjoying a conventional Thanksgiving meal. She does not think that they will appreciate hearing my traditional Thanksgiving speech about how the Pilgrims were guilty of committing mass genocide by giving their new Native American friends blankets filled with the smallpox virus, and that it is reprehensible that we, as a country, annually celebrate this rape and destruction of an entire culture.

Instead, my mother said, I should discuss more neutral topics, such as the weather.

I asked if it was all right if I discussed the astonishingly high rate of attendance at the Reykjavik opera house in Iceland (over ninety-eight per cent of the country's population has seen Tosca *at least once).*

My mother sighed and said, 'If you must,' which I take to be a sign that she is beginning to tire of hearing about Iceland.

Well, I am sorry, but I find Iceland extremely fascinating and I will not rest until I have visited the ice hotel.

9:45 a.m. – 11:45 a.m.

I watch the Macy's Thanksgiving Day parade with Mr Gianini Senior in what he calls the rec room.

They don't have rec rooms in Manhattan.

Just lobbies.

Remembering my mother's warning, I refrain from repeating another one of my traditional holiday rants – that the Macy's Thanksgiving Day parade is a gross example of American capitalism run amok. I mean, using cute animal-shaped balloons to lure children into begging their parents to buy them products that they don't need and the manufacturing of which is contributing to the destruction of our planet?

I am sorry, but that is just sick.

Besides, at one point during the broadcast I caught sight of Lilly standing in the crowd outside Office Max on Broadway and Thirty-Seventh, her video camera clutched to her slightly squished-in face (so much like a pug) as a float carrying Miss America and William Shatner of Star Trek *fame passed by. So I know Lilly is going to take care of denouncing Macy's on the next episode of her public access television show,* Lilly Tells It Like It Is *(every Friday night at nine, Manhattan cable channel 67).*

12:00 p.m.

Mr Gianini Junior's sister arrives with her husband, their two kids and the pumpkin pies. The kids, who are my age, are twins – a boy, Nathan, and a girl, Claire. I know right away that Claire and I are not going to get along, because when we are introduced she looks me up and down the way the cheerleaders do in the hallway at school and goes, in a very snotty voice, 'You're the one who's supposed to be a princess?'

And while I am perfectly aware that at five foot nine inches tall, with no visible breasts, feet the size of snowshoes, and hair that sits in a tuft on my head like the end of a cotton bud, I am the biggest freak in the freshman class of Albert Einstein High School For Boys (made co-educational circa 1975), I do not appreciate being reminded of it by

3

girls who do not even bother finding out that beneath this mutant façade beats the heart of a person who is only striving, just like everybody else in this world, to find self-actualization.

Not that I even care what Mr Gianini's niece Claire thinks of me. I mean, she is wearing a pony-skin miniskirt. And it is not even imitation pony-skin. She must know that a horse had to die just so she could have that skirt, but she obviously doesn't care.

Now Claire has pulled out her mobile phone and gone out on to the deck where the reception is best (even though it is thirty degrees outside, she apparently doesn't mind. She has that pony-skin to keep her warm, after all). She keeps looking in at me through the sliding glass doors and laughing as she talks on her phone.

I don't care. At least I am not wearing the skin of a murdered equine.

Nathan – who is dressed in baggy jeans and has a pager, in addition to a lot of gold jewellery – asks his grandfather if he can change the channel. So instead of traditional Thanksgiving viewing options, such as football or the Lifetime channel's made-for-TV movie marathon, we are now forced to watch MTV 2. Nathan knows all the songs and sings along with them. Most of them have dirty words that have been bleeped out, but Nathan sings them anyway.

1:00 p.m.
The food is served. We begin eating.

1:15 p.m.
We finish eating.

1:20 p.m.
I help Mrs Gianini clean up. She says not to be ridiculous and that I should go and 'have a nice gossip' with Claire.

It is frightening, if you think about it, how clueless old people can be sometimes.

Instead of going to have a nice gossip with Claire, I stay where I am

4

and tell Mrs Gianini how much I am enjoying having her son live with us. Mr G is very good about helping around the house and has even taken over my old job of cleaning the toilets. Not to mention the thirty-six-inch TV, pinball machine and foozball table he brought with him when he moved in.

Mrs Gianini is immensely gratified to hear this, you can just tell. Old people like to hear nice stuff about their kids, even if their kid, like Mr Gianini, is thirty-nine-and-a-half years old.

3:00 p.m.
We have to leave if we are going to beat the traffic home. I say goodbye. Claire does not say goodbye back to me, but Nathan does. He advises me to keep it real. Mrs Gianini gives us a lot of leftover turkey. I thank her, even though I don't eat turkey, being a vegetarian and am virulently opposed to the mass slaughter of helpless fowls every time a holiday rolls around.

6:30 p.m.
We finally make it back into the city, after spending three and a half hours in bumper-to-bumper traffic along the Long Island Expressway. Though there is nothing very express about it, if you ask me.

I barely have time to change into my baby-blue, floor-length Armani sheath dress and matching ballet flats before the limo honks downstairs and Lars, my bodyguard, arrives to escort me to my second Thanksgiving dinner.

7:30 p.m.
Arrive at the Plaza Hotel. I am greeted by the concierge, who announces me to the masses assembled in the Palm Court:

'Presenting Her Royal Highness Princess Amelia Mignonette Grimaldi Thermopolis Renaldo.'

God forbid he should just say Mia.

My father, the Prince of Genovia, and his mother, the Dowager

Princess, have rented the Palm Court for the evening in order to throw a Thanksgiving banquet for all of their friends. Despite my strenuous objections, Dad and Grandmere refuse to leave New York City until I have learned everything there is to know about being a princess . . . or until my formal introduction to the Genovian people the day before Christmas, whichever comes first. I have assured them that it isn't as if I am going to show up at the castle and start hurling olives at the ladies-in-waiting and scratching myself under the arms. I mean, I am fourteen years old – I do have some idea how to act, for crying out loud.

But Grandmere, at least, does not seem to believe this and so she is still subjecting me to daily princess lessons. Lilly recently contacted the United Nations to see whether these lessons constitute a human rights violation. She believes it is unlawful to force a minor to sit for hours practising tipping her soup bowl away from her – 'Always, always, away from you, Amelia!' – in order to scrape up a few drops of lobster bisque.

The UN has so far been unsympathetic to my plight, but that, I believe, is only because they have never actually met Grandmere. Were they to witness for themselves the frightful visage – made all the scarier by the fact that years ago Grandmere had her eyeliner permanently tattooed on to her lids, not to mention the fact that she shaves off her eyebrows every day and then draws on new ones in black pencil – hovering over me during these torture sessions, they'd send over a hostage negotiator before you could say Kofi Annan.

It was Grandmere's idea to have what she calls an 'old-fashioned' Thanksgiving dinner featuring mussels in a white wine sauce, squab stuffed with fois gras, lobster tails, and Iranian caviar, which you could never get before because of the embargo. She has invited two hundred of her closest friends, plus the Emperor of Japan and his wife, since they were in town anyway for a world trade summit.

That's why I had to wear ballet flats. Grandmere says it's rude to be taller than an emperor.

6

8:00 p.m. – 11:00 p.m.

I make polite conversation with the empress while we eat. Like me, she was just a normal person until one day she married the emperor and became royal. I, of course, was born royal. I just didn't know it until last October when my dad found out he couldn't have any more kids, due to his chemotherapy for testicular cancer having rendered him sterile. Then he had to admit he was actually a prince and all, and that though I am illegitimate, since my dad and my mom were never married, I am still the sole heir to the Genovian throne.

And even though Genovia is a very small country (population 50,000) crammed into a hillside along the Mediterranean Sea between Italy and France, it is still this very big deal to be princess of it.

Not a big enough deal for anyone to raise my allowance higher than ten dollars a week, apparently. But a big enough deal that I have to have a bodyguard follow me around everywhere I go just in case some Euro-trash terrorist with a ponytail and black leather trousers takes it into his head to kidnap me.

The empress knows all about this – what a bummer it is, I mean, being just a normal person one day and then having your face on the cover of People *magazine the next. She even gave me some advice: she told me I should always make sure my kimono is securely fastened before I raise my arm to wave to the populace.*

I thanked her, even though I don't actually own a kimono.

11:30 p.m.

I am so tired on account of having gotten up so early to go to Long Island, I have yawned in the empress's face twice. I have tried to hide these yawns the way Grandmere taught me to – by clenching my jaw and refusing to open my mouth. But this only makes my eyes water and the rest of my face stretch out like I am hurtling through a black hole. Grandmere gives me the evil eye over her salad with pears and walnuts, but it is no use. Even her malevolent stare cannot shake me from my state of extreme drowsiness.

Finally, my father notices and grants me a royal reprieve from dessert. Lars drives me back to the apartment. Grandmere is clearly upset because I am leaving before the cheese course. But it is either that or pass out in the fromage bleu. I know that in the end Grandmere will have retribution, undoubtedly in the form of forcing me to learn the names of every member of the Swedish royal family, or something equally heinous.

Grandmere always gets her way.

12:00 a.m.

After a long and exhausting day of giving thanks to the founders of our nation — those genocidal hypocrites known as the Pilgrims — I finally go to bed.

And that concludes Mia Thermopolis's Thanksgiving.

Saturday, December 5

Over.

That is what my life is. O-V-E-R.

I know I have said that before, but this time I really mean it.

And why? Why THIS TIME? Surprisingly, it's not because:

Two months ago I found out that I'm the heir to the throne of a small European nation, and that at the end of this month I am going to have to go to said small European nation and be formally introduced for the first time to the people over whom I will one day reign, and who will undoubtedly hate me, because given that my favourite shoes are my combat boots and my favourite TV show is *Baywatch*, I am so not the royal princess type.

Or because:

My mother, who is expecting to give birth to my Algebra teacher's child in approximately six months, recently eloped with said Algebra teacher.

Or even because:

At school they've been loading us down with so much homework – and after school, Grandmere's been torturing me so endlessly with all the princess stuff I've got to learn by Christmas – that I haven't even been able to keep up with this journal, let alone anything else.

Oh, no. It's not because of any of that. Why is my life over?

Because I have a boyfriend.

And, yes, at fourteen years of age, I suppose it's about time. I mean, all my friends have boyfriends. All of them, even Lilly, who blames the male sex for most, if not all, of society's ills.

And, OK, Lilly's boyfriend is Boris Pelkowski, who may, at the age of fifteen, be one of the nation's leading violin virtuosos, but that doesn't mean he doesn't tuck his sweater into his trousers, or that more often than not he doesn't have food in his braces. Not what I would call ideal boyfriend material, but Lilly seems to like him which is all that matters.

I guess.

I have to admit, when Lilly – possibly the pickiest person on this planet (and I should know, having been best friends with her since the first grade) – got a boyfriend and I still didn't have one, I pretty much started to think there was something wrong with me. You know, besides my gigantism and what Lilly's parents, the Drs Moscovitz, who are psychiatrists, call my inability to verbalize my inner rage.

And then, one day, out of the blue, I got one. A boyfriend, I mean.

Well, OK, not out of the blue. Kenny, from my Bio. class, started sending me all these anonymous love letters. I didn't know it was him. I kind of thought (OK, hoped) someone else was sending them. But in the end, it turned out to be Kenny. And by then I was in too deep, really, to get out. So *voilà*. I had a boyfriend.

Problem solved, right?

Not. So not.

It isn't that I don't like Kenny. I do. I really do. We have a lot in common. For instance, we both appreciate the preciousness of not just human, but *all* life forms, and refuse to dissect foetal pigs and frogs in Bio. Instead, we are writing term papers on the life cycles of various grub and mealworms.

And we both like science fiction. Kenny knows a lot more about it than I do, but he has been very impressed so far

10

by the extent of my familiarity with the works of Robert A. Heinlein and Isaac Asimov, both of whom we were forced to read in school (though he doesn't seem to remember this).

I haven't told Kenny that I actually find most science fiction boring, since there seems to be very few girls in it.

There are a lot of girl characters in Japanese anime, which Kenny also really likes, and which he has decided to devote his life to promoting (when he is not busy finding a cure for cancer). Unfortunately, I have noticed that most of the girls in Japanese anime seem to have misplaced their bras.

Plus I really think it might be detrimental to a fighter pilot to have a lot of long hair floating around in the cockpit while she is gunning down the forces of evil.

But like I said, I haven't mentioned any of this to Kenny. And mostly, we get along great. We have a fun time together. And in some ways, it's very nice to have a boyfriend, you know? Like, I don't have to worry now about not being asked to the Albert Einstein High School Non-Denominational Winter Dance (so-called because its former title, the Albert Einstein High School Christmas Dance, offended many of our non-Christmas-celebrating students).

And why is it that I do not have to worry about not being asked to the biggest dance of the school year, with the exception of prom?

Because I'm going with Kenny.

Well, OK, he hasn't exactly asked me yet, but he will. Because he is my boyfriend.

Isn't that great? Sometimes I think I must be the luckiest girl in the whole world. I mean, really. Think about it: I may not be pretty, but I am not grossly disfigured; I live in New

York City, the coolest place on the planet; I'm a princess; I have a boyfriend. What more could a girl ask for?

Oh, God.

WHO AM I KIDDING?????

This boyfriend of mine? Yeah, here's the scoop on him:

I DON'T EVEN LIKE HIM.

Well, OK, it's not that I don't like him. But this boyfriend thing, I just don't know. Kenny's a nice enough guy and all – don't get me wrong. I mean, he is funny and not boring to be with, certainly. And he's pretty cute, you know, in a tall, skinny sort of way.

It's just that when I see Kenny walking down the hall, my heart so totally doesn't start beating faster, the way girls' hearts start beating faster in those teen romances my friend Tina Hakim Baba is always reading.

And when Kenny takes my hand, at the movies or whatever, it's not like my hand gets all tingly in his, the way girls' hands do in those books.

And when he kisses me? Yeah, you know those fireworks people always talk about? OK, forget it about. No fireworks. Nil. *Nada*.

It's funny, because before I got a boyfriend I used to spend a lot of time trying to figure out how to get one and, once I got him, how I'd get him to kiss me.

But now that I actually have a boyfriend, mostly all I do is try to figure out how to get out of kissing him.

One way that I have found works quite effectively is the head turn. See, if you notice his lips coming towards you, you just turn your head at the last minute so all he gets is your cheek and maybe some hair.

I guess the worst thing is that when Kenny gazes deeply into my eyes – which he does a lot – and asks me what I am thinking about, I am usually thinking about this one certain person.

And that person isn't Kenny. It isn't Kenny at all. It is Lilly's older brother, Michael Moscovitz, whom I have loved for – oh, I don't know, MY ENTIRE LIFE.

Not that he even knows I am alive, except as his little sister's best friend, but whatever.

Which is why I have decided I have to tell him. Kenny, I mean. About how I really feel.

That's why my life is over. Because *how* do you say to somebody who wants to hold your hand in the movies that you don't like him in that way? Especially when he's already asked you out a bunch of times and you've gone. And you knew full well the whole time that he wasn't asking you as a friend – he was asking you as a potential life mate.

Or a royal consort, as Grandmere would say.

Wait, though. It gets worse.

Because now it's like everybody considers us this big item. You know? Now we're Kenny-and-Mia. Now, instead of Lilly and me hanging out together Saturday nights, it's Lilly-and-Boris and Kenny-and-Mia. Sometimes my friend Tina Hakim Baba, and her boyfriend, Dave Farouq El-Abar, and my other friend Shameeka Taylor, and her boyfriend, Daryl Gardner, join us, making it Lilly-and-Boris and Kenny-and-Mia and Tina-and-Dave and Shameeka-and-Daryl.

So if Kenny and I break up, not only will it be this very big deal, but who am I going to hang around with on Saturday nights? I mean, seriously. Lilly-and-Boris and Tina-and-Dave and Shameeka-and-Daryl won't want just plain Mia along. I'll be like this seventh wheel.

Not to mention, if Kenny and I break up, who will I go to the Non-Denominational Winter Dance with?

13

Oh, God, I have to go now. Lilly-and-Boris and Tina-and-Dave and Kenny and I are supposed to go ice-skating at the Rockefeller Center.

All I can say is, be careful what you wish for. It just might come true.

Saturday, December 5, 11 p.m.

OK, remember how I thought my life was over because I have a boyfriend now and I don't really like him in that way, and I have to break up with him without hurting his feelings, which is, I guess, probably impossible?

Yeah, well, I didn't know *how* over my life could actually be.

Not until last night, anyway.

That's right. Last night, when Lilly-and-Boris and Tina-and-Dave and Mia-and-Kenny were joined by a new couple, Michael-and-Judith.

That's right: Lilly's brother Michael showed up at the ice-skating rink, and he brought with him the president of the Computer Club – of which he is treasurer – Judith Gershner.

Judith Gershner, like Michael, is a senior at Albert Einstein High School. Judith Gershner, like Michael, is on the Honour Roll.

Judith Gershner, like Michael, will probably get into every college she applies to, because Judith Gershner, like Michael, is brilliant.

In fact, Judith Gershner, like Michael, won a prize last year at the Albert Einstein High School Annual Bio-Medical Technology Fair for her science project, in which she actually cloned a fruit fly.

She cloned a fruit fly. At home. In her *bedroom*.

Judith Gershner knows how to clone fruit flies in her bedroom. And me? Yeah, I can't even multiply fractions.

Hmm, gee, I don't know. If you were Michael Moscovitz – you know, a straight-A student who got into Columbia early decision – who would you rather go out with? A girl who can clone fruit flies in her bedroom, or a girl who is getting a D in Freshman Algebra, in spite of the fact that *her mother is married to her Algebra teacher*?

Not that there's even a chance of Michael ever asking me out. I mean, I have to admit, there were a couple of times when I thought he might. But that was clearly just wishful thinking on my part. I mean, why would a guy like Michael, who does really well in school and will probably excel at whatever career he ultimately chooses, ever ask out a girl like me, who would have flunked out of the ninth grade by now if it hadn't been for all those extra tutoring sessions with Mr Gianini and, ironically, Michael himself?

But Michael and Judith Gershner, on the other hand, are perfect for each other. Judith even looks like him, a little. I mean, they both have the same curly black hair and pale skin from being inside all the time, looking up stuff about genomes on the Internet.

But if Michael and Judith Gershner are so suited to one another, how come when I first saw them walking towards us while we were lacing up our rental skates, I got this very bad feeling inside?

I mean, I have absolutely no right to be jealous of the fact that Michael Moscovitz asked Judith Gershner to go skating with him. Absolutely no right at all.

Except that when I saw them together, I was shocked. I mean, Michael hardly ever leaves his room, on account of always being at his computer, maintaining his webzine, *Crackhead*. The last place I'd ever expected to see him is the ice-skating rink at Rockefeller Center during the height of the Christmas tree-lighting hysteria. Michael generally avoids places he considers tourists traps – like pretty much everywhere north of Bleecker Street.

But there he was. And there was Judith Gershner, in her overalls and Rockports and ski parka, chatting away about something – probably something really smart, like DNA.

I nudged Lilly in the side – she was lacing up her skates – and said, in this voice that I hoped didn't show what I was feeling inside, 'Look, there's your brother.'

And Lilly wasn't even surprised to see him! She looked over and went, 'Oh, yeah. He said he might show up.'

Show up with a *date*? Did he mention *that*? And would it have been too much for you, Lilly, to have mentioned this to me beforehand, so I could have had time for a little mental preparation?

Only Lilly doesn't know how I feel about her brother, so I guess it never occurred to her to break it to me gently.

Here's the subtle way in which I handled the situation. It was really smooth (NOT).

As Michael and Judith were looking around for a place to put on their skates:

Me: (*Casually, to Lilly*) I didn't know your brother and
           Judith Gershner were going out.
Lilly: (*Disgusted for some reason*) Please. They're not. She
           was just over at our place, working with Michael
           on some project for the stupid Computer Club.
           They heard we were all going skating, and Judith
           said she wanted to come too.
Me: Well, that sounds like they're going out to me.
Lilly: Whatever. Boris, must you constantly *breathe* on
           me?
Me: (*To Michael and Judith as they walk up to us*) Oh, hi,
           you guys. Michael, I didn't know you knew how to
           ice-skate.
Michael: (*Shrugging*) I used to be on a hockey team.
Lilly: (*Snorting*) Yeah, Pee Wee Hockey. That was before
           he decided that team sports were a waste of time

17

because the success of the team was dictated by the performance of all the players as a whole, as opposed to sports determined by individual performance such as tennis and golf.

Michael: Lilly, don't you ever shut up?

Judith: I love ice-skating! Although I'm not very good at it.

And she certainly isn't. Judith is such a bad skater, just to keep from falling flat on her face she had to hold on to both of Michael's hands while he skated backwards in front of her. I don't know which astonished me more – that Michael can skate backwards, or that he didn't seem to mind having to tow Judith all around the rink. I mean, I may not be able to clone a fruit fly, but at least I can remain upright unaided in a pair of ice-skates.

But Kenny really seemed to think Michael and Judith's method of skating was way preferable to skating the old-fashioned way – you know, solo – so he kept coming up and trying to tow me around the way Michael was towing Judith.

And even though I was all, 'Duh, Kenny, I know how to skate,' he said that wasn't the point. Finally, after he'd bugged me for like half an hour, I gave in, and let him hold both my hands as he skated in front of me, backwards.

Only the thing is, Kenny isn't very good at skating backwards. I can skate forward, but I'm not good enough at it that if someone is wobbling around in front of me, I can keep from crashing into him if he doesn't move out of the way fast enough.

Which was exactly what happened. Kenny fell down and I couldn't stop, so I crashed into him and my chin hit his knee and I bit my tongue and all this blood filled up in my mouth, and I didn't want to swallow it so I spat it out. Only unfortunately it went all over Kenny's jeans and on to the ice, which clearly impressed all of the tourists standing along the railings around the rink, taking pictures of their loved ones in front of the enormous Rockefeller Center Christmas tree, since they all turned around and started taking pictures of the girl spitting up blood on the ice below – a truly New York moment.

And then Lars came shooshing over – he is a champion ice-skater, thanks to his Nordic upbringing; quite a contrast to his bodyguard training in the heart of the Gobi desert – picked me up, looked at my tongue, gave me his handkerchief and told me to keep pressure on the wound. Then he said, 'That's enough skating for one night.'

And that was it. Now I've got this bloody gouge in the tip of my tongue, and it hurts to talk, and I was totally humiliated in front of millions of tourists, not to mention in front of my friends and, worst of all, Judith Gershner, who it turns out also got accepted early decision at Columbia (great, the same school Michael's going to in the fall) where she will be pre-med, and who advised me that I should see my family practitioner as it seemed likely to her that I might need stitches. In my *tongue*? I'm lucky, she said, I didn't bite the tip of it off.

Lucky!

Oh, yeah, I'll tell you how lucky I am:

I'm so lucky that while I lie here in bed writing this, with no one but my twenty-five pound cat, Fat Louie, to keep me company (and Fat Louie only likes me because I feed him), the boy I've been in love with since like for ever is up at midtown right now with a girl who knows how to clone fruit flies and can tell if wounds need stitches or not.

One good thing about this tongue thing, though: if Kenny was thinking about moving on to Frenching, we totally can't until I heal. And that could – according to Dr Fung, whom my mom called as soon as Lars brought me home – take anywhere from three to ten days.

Yes!

Ten Things I Hate about the
Holiday Season in New York City

1. Tourists who come in from out of town in their giant sports utility vehicles and try to run you over at the crosswalks, thinking they are driving like aggres-sive New Yorkers. Actually, they are driving like morons. Plus there is enough pollution in this city. Why can't they just take public transport, like normal people?

2. Stupid Rockefeller Center tree. They asked me to be the person who throws the switch to light it this year as I am considered New York's own royal in the press, but when I told them how cutting down trees contributes to the destruction of the ozone layer, they rescinded their invitation and had the mayor do it instead.

3. Stupid Christmas carols blaring from outside all the stores.

4. Stupid ice-skating with stupid boys who think they can skate backwards when they can't.

5. Stupid pressure to buy meaningful gifts for everyone you know.

6. Final exams.

7. Stupid, lousy New York weather. No snow, just cold wet rain, every single day. Whatever happened to a white Christmas? I'll tell you: global warming. You know why? Because everybody keeps driving SUVs and cutting down trees!

8. Stupid manipulative Christmas specials on TV.

9. Stupid manipulative Christmas commercials on TV.

10. Mistletoe. This stuff should be banned. In the hands of adolescent boys it becomes a societally approved

excuse to demand kisses. This is sexual harassment, if you ask me.

Plus all the wrong boys have it.

Sunday, December 6

Just got back from dinner at Grandmere's. All of my efforts to get out of having to go – even my pointing out that I am currently suffering from a perforated tongue – were in vain.

I could be bleeding out of the eyes and Grandmere would still expect me to show up for Sunday dinner.

And this one was even worse than usual. That's because Grandmere wanted to go over my itinerary for my trip to Genovia which, by the way, looks like this:

December 20
3 p.m.
Commencement of Royal
Duties
3:30 p.m. – 5 p.m.
Meet and greet palace staff
5 p.m. – 7 p.m.
Tour of palace
7 p.m. – 8 p.m.
Change for dinner
8 p.m. – 11 p.m.
Dinner with Genovian
dignitaries

December 21
8 a.m. – 9:30 a.m.
Breakfast with Genovian
public officials
10 a.m. – 11:30 a.m.
Tour of Genovian state
schools
12 p.m. – 1 p.m.
Meet with Genovian
schoolchildren
1:30 p.m. – 3 p.m.
Lunch with members of
Genovian Teachers'
Association
3:30 p.m. – 4:30 p.m.
Tour of Port of Genovia
and Genovian naval cruiser
(The Prince Philippe)
5 p.m. – 6 p.m.
Tour of Genovian General
Hospital

6 p.m. – 7 p.m.
Visit with hospital patients
7 p.m. – 8 p.m.
Change for dinner
8 p.m. – 11 p.m.
Dinner with Prince
Philippe, Dowager Princess,
Genovian military advisors

December 22
8 a.m. – 9 a.m.
Breakfast with members of
Genovian Olive Growers'
Association
10 a.m. – 11 a.m.
Christmas-tree lighting
ceremony, Genovia Palace
Courtyard
11:30 a.m. – 1:00 p.m.
Meet with Genovian
Historical Society

1 p.m. – 3 p.m.
Lunch with Genovian
Tourist Board
3:30 p.m. – 5:30 p.m.
Tour of Genovian National
Art Museum
6 p.m. – 7 p.m.
Visit Genovian War
Veterans Memorial,
place flowers on grave of
Unknown Soldier
7:30 p.m. – 8:30 p.m.
Change for dinner
8:30 p.m. – 11:30 p.m.
Dinner with Royal Family
of Monaco

And so on.

It all culminates in my appearance on my dad's annual nationally televised Christmas Eve address to the people of Genovia, during which he will introduce me to the populace. I am then supposed to make a speech about how thrilled I am to be Dad's heir, and how I promise to try to do as good a job as he has at leading Genovia into the twenty-first century.

Nervous? Me? About going on TV and promising 50,000 people that I won't let their country down?

Nah. Not me.

I just want to throw up every time I think about it, that's all.

Whatever. I so have nothing to look forward to. NOTHING. Not that I thought my trip to Genovia was going to be like going to Disneyland, but still. You'd think they'd have scheduled in *some* fun time. I'm not even asking for Mr Toad's Wild Ride. Just like some swimming or horseback riding.

But, apparently, there is not time for fun in Genovia.

As if going over my itinerary wasn't bad enough, I also had to spend my dinner at Grandmere's being nice to my cousin Sebastiano. Sebastiano Grimaldi is my dead grandfather's sister's daughter's kid. Which I guess actually makes him a cousin a couple times removed. But not removed enough that, if it weren't for me, he wouldn't be inheriting the throne to Genovia.

Seriously. If my dad had died without ever having had a kid, Sebastiano would be the next Prince of Genovia.

Maybe that's why my dad, every time he looks at Sebastiano, heaves this big shudder.

Or maybe it's just because my dad feels about Sebastiano the way I feel about my cousin Hank: I like him in theory, but in actual practice he kind of bugs me.

Sebastiano doesn't bug Grandmere, though. You can tell that Grandmere just loves him.

Which is really weird, because I always supposed Grandmere was incapable of loving anyone. Well, with the exception of Rommel, her miniature poodle.

But you can tell she totally adores Sebastiano. When she introduced him to me, and he bowed with this big flourish and kissed the air above my hand, Grandmere was practically beaming beneath her pink silk turban. Really.

I have never seen Grandmere beam before. Glare, plenty of times. But never beam.

Which might be why my dad started chewing the ice in his whiskey and soda in a very irritated manner. Grandmere's smile disappeared right away when she heard all that crunching.

'If you want to chew ice, Philippe,' Grandmere said, coldly, 'you can go and have your dinner at McDonald's with the rest of the proletariats.'

My dad stopped chewing his ice.

That's how scary Grandmere is. She can make princes stop chewing ice with one sentence.

It turns out Grandmere brought Sebastiano over from Genovia so that he could design my dress for my nationally televised introduction to my countrymen. Sebastiano is a very up-and-coming fashion designer – at least, according to Grandmere. She says it is important that Genovia supports its artists and craftspeople, or they will all flee to New York or, even worse, Los Angeles.

Which is too bad for Sebastiano, since he looks like the type who might really enjoy living in LA. He is thirtyish with long dark hair tied back in a ponytail, and is all tall and flamboyant-looking. Like, for instance, tonight, instead of a tie, Sebastiano was wearing a white silk ascot. And he had on a blue velvet jacket with leather trousers – which aren't any better, really, than pony-skin skirts, but at least we eat cows. Nobody eats ponies, except maybe in France.

I am fully prepared to forgive Sebastiano for the leather trousers if he designs me a dress that is nice enough. You know the kind of dress I mean. A dress that, should he happen to see me in it, will make Michael Moscovitz forget all about Judith Gershner and her fruit flies and fill his head with nothing but thoughts of me, Mia Thermopolis.

Only, of course, the chances of Michael ever actually seeing me in this dress are very slim, as my introduction to the Genovian people is only going to be on Genovian television, not CNN or anything.

Still, Sebastiano seemed ready to rise to the challenge. After dinner he even took out a pen and began sketching – right on the white tablecloth! – a design he thought might accentuate what he called my narrow waist and long legs.

Only, unlike my dad, who was born and raised in Genovia but speaks fluent English, Sebastiano doesn't have a real keen grasp of the language. He kept forgetting to put the second syllables on to words. So narrow became 'nar'. Just like 'coffee' became 'coff', and when he described something as magical, it came out as 'madge'. Even the butter wasn't safe. When Sebastiano asked me to please pass him the 'butt', I had to stuff my napkin in my mouth to keep from laughing out loud.

It didn't do any good, though, since Grandmere caught me and, raising one of her drawn-on eyebrows, went, 'Amelia, kindly do not make light of other people's speech habits. Your own are not even remotely perfect.'

Which is certainly true, considering the fact that, with my swollen tongue, I can't really say any word that starts with *s*.

Not only did Grandmere not mind Sebastiano saying the word 'butt' at the dinner table, she didn't mind his drawing on the tablecloth, either. She looked down at his sketch and said, 'Brilliant. Simply brilliant. As usual.'

Sebastiano looked very pleased. 'Do you real think so?' he asked.

Only I didn't think his sketch was so brilliant. It just looked like an ordinary dress to me. Certainly nothing to make anyone forget the fact that I'm about as likely to clone a fruit fly as I am to eat a Quarter Pounder with cheese.

'Um,' I said. 'Can't you make it a little more . . . I don't know. Sexy?'

Grandmere and Sebastiano exchanged looks. 'Sexy?' Grandmere echoed, with an evil laugh. 'How? By making it lower-cut? But you haven't got anything there to show!'

Now, seriously. I would expect to hear this kind of thing from the cheerleaders at school, who have made demeaning other people – especially me – a sort of new Olympic sport. But what kind of person says things like this to her only grandchild? I had meant, of course, a side slit, or maybe some fringe. I wasn't asking for anything Jennifer Lopez-ish.

But trust Grandmere to turn it into something like that. Why can't I have a normal grandmother, who bakes me cookies and can't stop bragging to her friends in the Bridge Club about how wonderful I am? Why do I have to be cursed with a grandmother who shaves off her eyebrows and seems to enjoy making light of my inadequacies?

It was while Grandmere and Sebastiano were cackling to themselves over this great witticism at my expense that my dad abruptly got up and left the table, saying he had to make a call. I suppose it's every man for himself where Grandmere is concerned, but you would think my own father would stick up for me once in a while.

I don't know, maybe it was residual depression over the giant hole in my tongue (which doesn't even have a nice sterling silver stud in it so I can pretend to have done it on purpose to be controversial). But as I sat there listening to Grandmere and Sebastiano chatter away about how pathetic it was that I would never be able to wear anything strapless, unless some miracle of nature occurred one night that inflated me from a 32A to a 34C, I couldn't help thinking about Michael.

Like about how with my luck, Michael will end up marrying Judith Gershner, so that even if I do ever get the guts to break up with Kenny, I will still never get a chance to be with the man I truly love.

And probably, given my luck, it will turn out that Sebastiano isn't just in town to design me a dress for my royal introduction, but to kill me so that he can assume the throne of Genovia himself.

Or, as Sebastiano would say, 'ass' the throne.

Seriously. That kind of stuff happens on *Baywatch* all the time. You wouldn't believe the number of royal family members Mitch has had to save from assassination.

Like supposing I put on the dress that Sebastiano has designed for me to wear when I'm introduced to the people of Genovia and it ends up squeezing me to death, just like that corset Snow White puts on in the original version of her story by the Brothers Grimm. You know, the part they left out of the Disney movie because it was too gruesome.

Anyway, what if the dress squeezes me to death and then I'm lying in my coffin, looking all pale and queenly, and Michael comes to my funeral and ends up gazing down at me and doesn't realize until right then that he has always loved me?

Then he'll *have* to break up with Judith Gershner.

Hey. It could happen.

OK, well, probably not, but thinking about that was better than listening to Grandmere and Sebastiano talk about me as if I wasn't even there.

I was roused from my pleasant little fantasy about Michael pining for me for the rest of his life by Sebastiano saying suddenly, 'She has bute bone struck,' which, when I realized I was the *she* he was referring to, I took to be a compliment about my bone structure.

29

Only a second later it wasn't such a compliment when he went, 'I put make-up on her that make her look like a mod.'

Which, of course, is insulting because a nice person would say that I already look like a model (although of course I don't).

Grandmere certainly wasn't about to come to my defence, however. She was feeding bits of her leftover veal marsala to Rommel, who was sitting on her lap shivering as usual since all of his fur fell out due to canine allergies.

'I wouldn't count on her father letting you,' she said to Sebastiano. 'Philippe is hopelessly old-fashioned.'

Which is so the pot calling the kettle black! I mean, Grandmere still thinks that cats go around trying to suck the breath out of their owners while they are sleeping. Seriously. She is always trying to convince me to give Fat Louie away.

So while Grandmere was going on about how old-fashioned her son is, I got up and joined him on the balcony.

He was checking his messages on his mobile. He's supposed to play racquetball tomorrow with the prime minister of France, who is in town for the same summit as the Emperor of Japan.

'Mia,' he said, when he saw me. 'What are you doing out here? It's freezing. Go back inside.'

'I will in a minute,' I said. I stood there next to him and looked out over the city. It really is kind of awe-inspiring, the view of Manhattan from the penthouse of the Plaza Hotel. I mean, you look at all those lights in all those windows and you think, for each light there's probably at least one person, but maybe even more, maybe even like ten people, and that's, well, pretty mind-boggling.

I've lived in Manhattan my whole life but it still impresses me.

Anyway, while I was standing there, looking at all the

lights, I suddenly realized that one of them probably belonged to Judith Gershner. Judith was probably sitting in her room right this moment cloning something new. A pigeon or whatever. I got yet another flash of her and Michael looking down at me after I'd split open my tongue. Hmm, let me see: girl who can clone things, or girl who bit her own tongue? I don't know, which girl would *you* choose?

My dad must have noticed something was wrong, since he went, 'Look, I know Sebastiano is a bit much, but just put up with him for the next couple of weeks. For my sake.'

'I wasn't thinking about Sebastiano,' I said sadly.

My dad made this grunting noise but he made no move to go back inside, even though it was about forty degrees out there and my dad, well, he's completely bald. I could see that the tips of his ears were getting red with cold, but still he didn't budge. He didn't even have a coat on – just one of his ubiquitous charcoal-grey Armani suits.

I figured this was invitation enough to go on. You see, ordinarily my dad is not who I would go to first if I had a problem. Not that we're not close. It's just that, you know, he's a guy. What does he know about teenage girls?

On the other hand, he's had a lot of experience in the romance department so I figured he might just be able to offer some insight into this particular dilemma.

'Dad,' I said. 'What do you do if you like someone but they don't, you know, know it?'

My dad went, 'If Kenny doesn't know you like him by now then I'm afraid he's never going to get the message. Haven't you been out with him every weekend since Halloween?'

This is the problem with having a bodyguard who is on your father's payroll: all of your personal business totally gets discussed behind your back.

31

'I'm not talking about Kenny, Dad,' I said. 'It's someone else. Only like I said, he doesn't know I like him.'

'What's wrong with Kenny?' my dad wanted to know. 'I like Kenny.'

Of course my dad likes Kenny. Because the chances of me and Kenny ever getting past first base are like nil. What father doesn't want his teenage daughter to date a guy like that?

But if my dad has any serious hope of keeping the Genovian throne in the hands of the Renaldos and not allowing it to slip into Sebastiano's control, he had better get over the whole Kenny thing, because I'm pretty sure that Kenny and I will not be doing any procreating. In this lifetime, anyway.

'Dad,' I said. 'Forget Kenny, OK? Kenny and I are just friends. I'm talking about someone else.'

My dad was looking over the side of the balcony railing, like he wanted to spit. Not that he ever would. I don't think. 'Do I know him? This someone else, I mean?'

I hesitated. I've never really admitted to anyone out loud that I have a crush on Michael. Really. I mean, who could I tell? Lilly would just make fun of me – or worse, tell him. And Mom, well, she's got her own problems.

'It's Lilly's brother,' I said, in a rush, to get it over with.

My dad looked alarmed. 'Isn't he in college?'

'Not yet,' I said. 'He's going in the fall.' When he still looked alarmed, I said, 'Don't worry, Dad. I don't stand a chance. Michael is very smart. He'd never want someone like me.'

Then my dad got all offended. It was like he couldn't figure out which to be, worried about my liking a senior, or angry that the senior didn't like me back.

'What do you mean, he'd never want someone like you?' my father demanded. 'What's wrong with you?'

'Duh, Dad,' I said. 'I practically flunked Algebra, remember? Michael is going to an Ivy League school in the fall, for crying out loud. What would he want with a girl like me?'

Now my dad was *really* annoyed. 'You may take after your mother as far as your aptitude with numbers is concerned, but you take after me in every other respect.'

This was surprising to hear. I stuck out my chin and tried to believe it. 'Yeah,' I said.

'And you and I, Mia, are not unintelligent,' my dad went on. 'If you want this Michael fellow, you must let him know it.' My dad looked at all the lights stretched out before us before going on in a different voice, 'Do not make the mistake I have in the past, Mia, of keeping your feelings to yourself, out of shyness . . . or worse, pride.'

I looked up at my dad kind of sharply at that. Because something in his voice . . . I don't know. He just sounded so . . . sad. Was he, I couldn't help wondering, talking about Mom? Like he wished that, before she'd married Mr Gianini, he had said something to her about how he felt about her? I mean about how he *really* felt about her – not about her leaving the electricity bills in the salad spinner, but about how he *really* felt, deep down?

I think maybe so. Especially when he looked down at me – my dad's not super tall, you know, for a guy, but he's taller than me, anyway – and went, with his eyelids kind of crinkling up at the corners, 'Faint heart never won fair lady, you know, Mia.'

I didn't know what to say to that. I mean, how is a person supposed to reply to something like that?

Not that it ever would have worked out between them, whatever Dad might think. I mean, Mom would so never have fitted in back at the palace, given her enthusiasm for *World's Scariest Police Car Chases* (which I'm sure they don't have in Genovia) and her love of jalapeno nachos (ditto). She would have grown resentful and then made my dad's life a never-ending misery.

At least this way, he still gets to date Victoria's Secret underwear models.

So instead of saying anything like, 'Gee, Dad, sorry it didn't work out between you and Mom,' which would, of course, have been a lie, I just went, 'You think I should just go up to Michael and be like, "Hey, I like you"?'

My dad shook his head in disgust. 'No, no, no,' he said. 'Of course you must be more subtle than that. Tell him by *showing* how you feel.'

'Oh,' I said. I may take after my father in every respect except my maths aptitude, but I had no idea what he was talking about. I kept seeing this picture in my head of me showing Michael how I felt about him by thrusting my tongue into his mouth in the hallway at school when I passed him between English and lunch – a kind of painful prospect, under the circumstances.

'We'd better get back in,' my father said. 'Or your grand-mother will suspect us of plotting against her.'

So what else is new? Grandmere is always suspecting somebody of plotting against her. She thinks the launderers at the Plaza are plotting against her. She blames the soap they use on their linens for making all of Rommel's fur fall out.

Reminded of plots, I asked my dad, 'Do you think Sebastiano's plotting to kill me so he can ascend the throne himself?'

My dad made a strangled noise, but he managed not to

burst out laughing. I guess that wouldn't have seemed very princely.

'No, Mia,' he said. 'I do not.'

But my dad, he really doesn't have much of an imagination. I have decided to stay on the alert about Sebastiano, just in case.

My mom just poked her head into my room to say that Kenny is on the phone for me.

I suppose he wants to ask me to the Non-Denominational Winter Dance. Really, it is about time.

OK. I am in shock. Kenny so did NOT ask me to the Non-Denominational Winter Dance. Instead, this is how our conversation went:

Me: Hello?

Kenny: Hi, Mia. It's Kenny.

Me: Oh, hi, Kenny. What's the matter?

   Kenny sounded funny, which is why I asked.

Kenny: Well, I just wanted to see if you were OK. I mean, if your tongue was OK.

Me: It's a little better, I guess.

Kenny: Because I was really worried. You know. I really, really didn't mean to pull you down like that.

Me: Kenny, I know. It was just an accident.

   This is when I started realizing I'd asked my dad the wrong question. I should have asked him what's the best way to break up with somebody, not what's the best way to let someone know you like them.

   Anyway, to get back to what Kenny said:

Kenny: Well, I just wanted to call and wish you a good night. And say that I hope you feel better. And also to let you know . . . well, Mia, that I love you.

Me: ⸻

   I didn't say anything right away, because I was completely FREAKED OUT!!!!

   It wasn't exactly as if it happened out of the blue, because we are sort of going out, after all.

   But still, what kind of guy calls a girl on the phone and says *I love you*??? Except for weird psycho stalkers? And Kenny's not a weird psycho stalker. He's just Kenny. So what's he doing calling me on the phone and telling me he loves me????

And then, brilliant me, here's what I do. Because he was still on the phone, waiting for an answer and all. So I go:

Me: Um, OK.

Um, OK.

A boy says he loves me and this is how I respond: *Um, OK*. Oh, yeah, good thing my future career lies in the diplomatic corps.

So then, poor Kenny, he's like waiting for some response other than *Um, OK*, as anybody would.

But I am perfectly incapable of giving him one. Instead, I just go:

Me: Well, see you tomorrow.

AND I HUNG UP!!!!!

Oh my God, I am the meanest, most ungrateful girl in the world. After Sebastiano kills me, I am going to burn in hell.

Seriously.

To Do Before Leaving for Genovia

1. Detailed list for Mom and Mr G: how to care for Fat Louie while I am away.
2. Stock up on cat food, litter.
3. Christmas/Hanukkah presents! For:
   Mom – electric breast pump? Check this.
   Mr G – new drum sticks.
   Dad – book on vegetarianism. He should eat better if he wants to keep his cancer in remission.
   Lilly – what she always wants, blank videotapes for her show.
   Lars – see if Prada makes a shoulder holster that would fit his Glock.
   Kenny – gloves? Something NON-romantic.
   Fat Louie – catnip ball.
   Grandmere – what do you get for the woman who has everything, including an eighty-nine carat sapphire pendant given to her by the Sultan of Brunei? Soap on a rope?
4. Break up with Kenny . . . only how can I? He LOVES me.

Only not enough to ask me to the Non-Denominational Winter Dance, I've noticed.

Monday, December 7, Homeroom

Lilly doesn't believe me about Kenny calling and saying he loves me. I told her in the car on the way to school this morning (thank God Michael had a dentist appointment and wasn't there. I would sooner die than discuss my love life in front of him. It's bad enough having to discuss it in front of my bodyguard. If I had to discuss it in front of this person I've been worshipping for half my life, I think I'd probably go completely borderline personality disorder)

Anyway, so Lilly went, 'I categorically refuse to believe Kenny would do something like that.'

'Lilly,' I said. I had to keep my voice down so the driver wouldn't hear, up in the front seat. 'I am dead serious. He told me he loves me. *I love you.* That is what he said. It was completely random and weird.'

'He probably didn't say that. He probably said something else and you misunderstood him.'

'Oh, what? I *glove* you?'

'Well, of course not,' Lilly said. 'That doesn't even make any sense.'

'Well, then what? What could Kenny have said that sounded like I love you, but wasn't I love you?'

Lilly got mad then. She went, 'You know, you have been acting weird about Kenny for the past month. Since the two of you started going out, practically. I don't know what's wrong with you. All I ever heard before was "Why don't I have a boyfriend? How come everybody I know has a boyfriend but me? When am I going to get a boyfriend?" but now you've got one, you aren't the least bit appreciative of him.'

Even though what she was saying was true, I acted

offended because I have been trying really hard not to let the fact that I am not in love with Kenny show.

'That is so false,' I said. 'I completely appreciate Kenny.'

'Oh, yeah? I think the truth of the matter is, you, Mia, simply aren't ready to have a boyfriend.'

Boy did I see red after *that* remark.

'*Me*? Not ready to have a boyfriend? Are you kidding? I've been waiting my whole life to have a boyfriend!'

'Well, if that's true' – Lilly was looking very superior – 'why won't you let him kiss you on the lips?'

'Where did you hear *that*?' I demanded.

'Kenny told Boris, of course, who told me.'

'Oh, great,' I said, trying to remain calm. 'So now our boyfriends are talking about us behind our backs. And you're condoning this?'

'Of course not,' Lilly said. 'But I do find it intriguing, from a psychological point of view.'

This is the problem with being best friends with someone whose parents are psychiatrists. Everything you do is interesting to them from a psychological point of view.

'Where I let anybody kiss me,' I exploded, 'is *my* business! Not yours, and not Boris's, either.'

'Well,' Lilly said. 'I'm just saying, if Kenny did say what you say he said – you know, the L word – then maybe he said it because he can't express the depths of his feelings any other way. You know. Other than *verbally*. Since you won't let him, *physically*.'

So I suppose that, technically, I should be thankful that Kenny chose merely to *say* the words 'I love you', rather than enacting them physically, which, God knows, might have actually have involved his tongue.

Oh, God, I don't even want to think about it any more.

Monday, December 7, Still Homeroom

They just passed out the Final Exam schedules. Here is mine:

FINAL EXAM SCHEDULE
December 14 – Reading Day
December 15 – Periods One and Two

For me, that means the Algebra and English finals will be on the same day. But that's OK. I'm doing pretty good in English. Well, except for that sentence diagramming thing. As if I'll ever need to do that in my future role as princess of the smallest nation in Europe.

Algebra, unfortunately, I am told I will probably need to know. DAMN!

December 16 – Periods Three and Four
World Civ.: easy. I mean, Grandmere has told me enough stories about post-World War Two Europe for me to pass any test. I probably know more about it than the teacher. And PE? How can you give a Final in PE? We already had the Presidential Fitness Test (I passed everything but chin-ups).

December 17 – Periods Five, Six, and Seven
Gifted and Talented? No exam there. They don't give finals in classes that are basically study hall. That will be a snap. I have French seventh period. I do OK in oral, not so great in written. Fortunately Tina's in the same class. Maybe we can study together.

But I have Bio. sixth period. That won't be so easy. The only reason I'm not flunking Bio. is because of Kenny. He slips me most of the answers.

41

And if I break up with him, that will be the end of that.

December 18 – Non-Denominational Winter Carnival and Dance

The Winter Carnival should be fun. All the different school clubs and stuff are going to have booths, with traditional winter fare, like hot cider. This will be followed in the evening by the dance I am supposed to go to with Kenny. If he ever asks me to it, I mean.

Unless, of course, I do the right thing and break up with him.

In which case, I won't be able to go at all, because you can't go without a date.

I wish Sebastiano would just hurry up and kill me already.

Monday, December 7, Algebra

WHY???? WHY can't I ever remember my Algebra note-book?????

FIRST – Evaluate exponents
SECOND – Multiply and divide in order left to right
THIRD – Perform addition and subtraction in order left to right
EXAMPLE: $2 \times 3 - 15/5 = 6 - 3 = 3$

Oh, God. Lana Weinberger just tossed me a note.

What now? This can't be good. Lana's had it in for me for ever. Don't ask me why. I mean, I could kind of understand her resenting me for when Josh Richter asked me to the Cultural Diversity Dance instead of her. But he only asked me because of the princess thing – and they got back together right after. Besides, Lana hated me long before that.

When I open the note, guess what it says:

I heard what happened to you at the skating rink this weekend. Guess the BF is going to have to wait a little longer if he wants to see any tongue action, huh?

Oh my God. Does *everyone* in the entire school know that Kenny and I have not yet French kissed?

It is all Kenny's fault, of course.

What next? The cover of the *Post*?

I'm telling you, if our parents knew what actually goes on every day in the typical American high school, they would totally opt for home-schooling.

43

Monday, December 7, World Civ.

It is clear what I have to do.

I've always known it, of course, and if it hadn't been for, you know, the dance, I would have done it long before now.

But it is clear now that I cannot afford to wait until after the dance. I should have done it last night when he called, but you can't really do something like that over the phone. Well, I mean, a girl like Lana Weinberger probably could, but not me.

No, I don't think I can put it off another day: I have got to break up with Kenny. I simply cannot continue living this lie.

Fortunately, I do have the support of at least one person in this plan: Tina Hakim Baba.

I didn't want to tell her. I didn't plan on telling anybody. But it all sort of slipped out today in the Girls' Room between third and fourth periods while Tina was putting on her eye make-up. Her dad won't let her wear make-up, you see, so Tina has to wait until she gets to school to put it on. She has a deal with her bodyguard, Wahim (Tina has a bodyguard too, just like me, but not because she's a princess, it's because her dad is a rich oil sheik and he is paranoid someone is going to kidnap her and hold her for ransom). The deal is that Tina won't tell her parents how much Wahim flirts with Mademoiselle Klein, our French teacher, if Wahim doesn't tell Mr and Mrs Hakim Baba about Tina's Maybelline addiction.

Anyway, all of a sudden I just couldn't take it any more, and I ended up telling Tina what Kenny said last night on the phone—

And a lot more than that actually.

But first the part about Kenny's phone call.

44

Unlike Lilly, *Tina* believed me.

But Tina also had the totally wrong reaction. She thought it was great.

'Oh my God, Mia, you are so lucky,' she kept saying. 'I wish Dave would tell me he loves me! I mean, I know he is fully committed to our relationship, but his idea of romance is paying to have my fries super-sized at Mickey D's.'

This was so not the kind of support I was looking for.

'But, Tina,' I said. I felt Tina, with her extensive romance reading, would understand. 'The thing is, I don't love him.'

Tina widened her mascaraed eyes at me. 'You don't?'

'No,' I said, miserably. 'I mean, I really like him, as a friend. But I'm not in love or anything. Not with him.'

'Oh, God,' Tina said, reaching out and grabbing my wrist. 'There's someone else, isn't there?'

We only had a few minutes before the bell rang. We both had to get to class.

And yet, for some reason, I chose this moment to make my big confession. I don't know why. It's just that I can't stop thinking about what my dad said. You know, about showing the guy I like how I feel. Tina, I felt, was the only person I knew who would know how to help me do that.

So I went, 'Yes.'

Tina nearly spilled her cosmetic bag, she was so excited.

'I knew it!' she yelled. 'I knew there was a reason you wouldn't let him kiss you!'

My jaw dropped. '*You* know about that too?'

'Well.' Tina shrugged. 'Kenny told Dave, who told me.'

Jeez! What's that Oprah's always complaining about – about how men aren't in touch with their emotions and don't share enough? It sounds to me like Kenny's been doing enough sharing recently to make up for several centuries worth of masculine reticence.

'So who is he?' Tina asked, all eagerly, as she packed up her eyelash curler and lip-liner. 'The guy you like?'

I went, 'It doesn't matter. Besides, the whole thing is completely futile. He sort of has a girlfriend, I think.'

Tina whipped her head around to look at me, making her thick black braid smack her in her own face, which is chubby, but in a good way.

'It's Michael, isn't it?' she demanded, grabbing my arm again. She was holding on so tight, it hurt.

My instinctive reaction, of course, was to deny it. In fact, I even opened my mouth, all set to have the word 'no' come out of it.

But then I was like, Why? Why should I deny it to Tina? Tina wouldn't tell anyone. And she might be able to help me.

So instead of saying No, I took a deep breath and said, 'If you tell anyone, I'll kill you, understand? KILL YOU.'

Tina did a strange thing then. She let go of my arm and started jumping up and down in a circle.

'I knew it, I knew it, I knew it,' she said as she jumped. Then she stopped jumping and grabbed my arm again. 'Oh, Mia, I always thought you two would make the cutest couple. I mean, I like Kenny and all, but he's, you know.' She wrinkled up her nose. 'No Michael.'

If I had thought it felt strange last night telling my dad the truth about my feelings for Michael, that was nothing – NOTHING – compared to how it felt to be telling someone my own age. The fact that Tina hadn't burst out laughing or gone, 'Yeah, right,' in a sarcastic way meant more to me than I ever would have expected.

And the fact that she seemed to understand – even

applaud – my feelings for Michael made me want to fling my arms around her and give her a great big hug.

Only there was no time for that since the bell was about to ring.

Instead, I gushed, 'Really? You really don't think it's stupid?'

'Duh,' Tina said. 'Michael is *hot. And* he's a senior.' Then she looked troubled. 'But what about Kenny? And Judith?'

'I know,' I said, my shoulders slumping in a manner that would have caused Grandmere to rap me on the back of the head, if she'd seen them. 'Tina, I don't know what to do.'

Tina's dark eyebrows furrowed with concentration.

'I think I read a book where this happened once,' she said. '*Love's Tender Storm*, it was called, I think. If I could just remember how they resolved everything—'

But before she could remember, the bell rang. We were both totally late to class.

But, if you ask me, it was worth it. Because now, at least, I don't have to worry alone. I have somebody else worrying with me.

Monday, December 7, Gifted and Talented

Lunch was a disaster.

Considering that everybody in the entire school seems to know, in the minutest detail, exactly what I've been doing – or not doing – with my tongue lately, I guess I shouldn't have been surprised. But it was even worse than I could have imagined.

That's because I ran into Michael at the salad bar. I was creating my usual chickpea and pinto bean pyramid when I saw him headed for the burger grill (despite my best efforts, both Moscovitzes remain stubbornly carnivorous).

Seriously, all I did was say 'Fine' when he asked how I was doing. You know, on account of how last time he saw me I was bleeding from the mouth (what a nice picture that must have been. I am so glad that I have been able to maintain an appearance of dignity and beauty at all times in front of the man I love).

Anyway, then I asked him, just to be polite, you know, how his dentist appointment went. It's not my fault, what happened next.

Which was that Michael started telling me about how he'd had to have this cavity filled and that his lips were still numb from the novocaine. Seeing as how I have experienced a certain amount of sensation-deadening, what with my gouged tongue, I could relate to this, so I just sort of, you know, *looked* at Michael's lips while he was talking, which I have never really done before. I mean, I have looked at other parts of Michael's body (particularly when he comes into the kitchen in the morning with no shirt on, like he does every time I sleep over at Lilly's). But I've never really looked at his lips. You know. Up close.

Michael actually has very nice lips. Not thin lips, like

mine. I don't know if you should say this about a boy's lips, but Michael's look like if you kissed them, they'd be very soft.

It was while I was noticing this about Michael's lips that the very bad thing happened: I was looking at them, you know, and wondering if they'd be soft to kiss and, as I looked, I sort of actually pictured us kissing, you know, in my head. And right then I got this very warm feeling – the one they talk about in Tina's romance novels – and RIGHT THEN was when Kenny went by on his way to get his usual lunch, Coke and an ice-cream sandwich.

I know Kenny can't read my mind – if he could, he totally would have broken up with me by now – but maybe he caught some hint as to what I was thinking, and that's why he didn't say 'hi' back when Michael and I said 'hi'.

Well, that and the whole part where I said *Um, OK* after he said he loved me.

Kenny must have known something was up, if my face was anywhere near as red-hot as it felt. Maybe *that's* why he didn't say 'hi' back. Because I was looking so guilty. I'd certainly *felt* guilty. I mean, there I was, looking at another guy's lips and wondering what it would be like to kiss them, and my boyfriend goes walking by.

I am so going to bad-girl hell when I die.

You know what I wish? I wish everyone *could* read my mind. Because then Kenny would never have asked me out. He'd have known I don't think of him that way. And Lilly wouldn't make fun of me for not letting Kenny kiss me. She would know the reason I don't is that I'm in love with someone else.

The bad part is, she'd know who that someone else is.

And that someone probably wouldn't even speak to me again, because it's totally uncool for a senior to go out with a freshman. Especially one who can't go anywhere without a bodyguard.

Besides, I'm almost positive he's going out with Judith Gershner, because after he came back from the grill, he went and sat down next to her.

So that settles that.

I wish I were leaving for Genovia tomorrow instead of in two weeks.

Monday, December 7, French

In spite of that disastrous incident at lunch, I had a pretty good time in Gifted and Talented. In fact, it was almost like old times again. I mean, before we all started going out with each other and everyone became so obsessed with the inner workings of my mouth, and all that.

It was really nice. Mrs Hill spent the whole class period in the teachers' lounge across the hall, yelling at American Express on the phone, leaving us free to do what we usually do during her class . . . whatever we wanted. For instance, those of us who, like Lilly's boyfriend Boris, wanted to work on our individual projects (Boris is learning to play some new sonata on his violin) which is what Gifted and Talented class is supposedly for, did so.

Those of us, however, like Lilly and me, who did not want to work on our individual projects (mine is studying for Algebra; Lilly's is working on her cable access TV show) did not.

This was especially satisfying because Lilly had completely forgotten about the whole kissing thing between Kenny and me. The reason for this is that now she's mad at Mrs Spears, her Honours English teacher, who shot down her term paper proposal.

It really was unfair of Mrs Spears to turn it down, because it was actually very well thought out and quite creative. Here is a copy of it I made:

How to Survive High School
by Lilly Moscovitz

Having spent the past two months locked into that institution of secondary education commonly referred to as high school, I feel that I am a qualified authority on the subject. From pep rallies to morning announcements, I have observed high school life and all of its complexities. Sometime in the next four years I will be granted my freedom from this festering hellhole, and then I will publish my carefully compiled High School Survival Guide.

Little did my peers and teachers know that as they went about their daily routines, I was recording their activities for study by future generations. With my handy guide, every ninth grader's sojourn in high school can be a little more fruitful. Students of the future will learn that the way to settle their differences with their peers is not through violence, but through the sale of a really scathing screenplay – featuring characters based on those very individuals who tormented them all those years – to a major Hollywood movie studio. That, not a Molotov cocktail, is the path to true glory.

Here, for your reading pleasure, are a few examples of the topics I will explore in 'How to Survive High School', by Lilly Moscovitz:
1. High School Romance: Or, I cannot open my locker because two oversexed adolescents are leaning up against it, making out.

2. Cafeteria food: Can corndogs legally be listed as a meat product?
3. How to communicate with the subhuman individuals who populate the hallways.
4. Guidance Counsellors: Who do they think they're kidding?
5. Get Ahead by Forging: The Art of the Hall Pass

Does that sound good, or what? Now look what Mrs Spears had to say about it:

Lilly – Sorry as I am to hear that your experience thus far at AEHS has not been a positive one, I am afraid I am going to have to make it worse by asking you to find another topic for your term paper. A for creativity, as usual, however. Mrs Spears

Can you believe that? Talk about unfair! Lilly's been censored! By rights, her proposal ought to have brought the school's administration to its knees. Lilly says she is appalled by the fact that, considering how much our tuition costs, this is the kind of support we can expect from our teachers. Then I reminded her that this isn't true of Mr Gianini, who really goes beyond the call of duty by staying after school every day to conduct help sessions for people like me who aren't doing so well in Algebra.

Lilly says Mr Gianini probably only started pulling that staying-after-school thing so that he could ingratiate himself with my mother, and now he can't stop because then she'll realize it was all just a set-up and divorce him.

I don't believe that, however. I think Mr G would have stayed after school to help me whether he was dating my mom or not. He's that kind of guy.

Anyway, the upshot of it all is that now Lilly is launching

another one of her famous campaigns. This is actually a good thing, as it will keep her mind off me and where I am putting (or not putting) my lips. Here's how it started:

Lilly: The real problem with this school isn't the teachers. It's the apathy of the student body. For instance, let's say we wanted to stage a walkout.

Me: A walkout?

Lilly: You know. We all get up and walk out of the school at the same time.

Me: Just because Mrs Spears turned down your term paper proposal?

Lilly: No, Mia. Because she's trying to usurp our individuality by forcing us to bend to corporate feudalism. Again.

Me: Oh. And how is she doing that?

Lilly: By censoring us when we are at our most creatively fertile.

Boris: (*Leaning out of the supply closet, where Lilly made him go when he started practising his latest sonata*): Fertile? Did someone say fertile?

Lilly: Get back in the closet, Boris. Michael, can you send a mass e-mail tonight to the entire student body, declaring a walkout tomorrow at ten?

Michael: (*Who was working on the booth he and Judith Gershner and the rest of the Computer Club are going to have up at the Winter Carnival*) I can, but I won't.

Lilly: WHY NOT?

Michael: Because it was your turn to empty the dishwasher last night, but you weren't home so I had to do it.

Lilly: But I TOLD Mom I had to go down to the studio to edit the last few finishing touches on this week's show!

Lilly's TV programme, *Lilly Tells It Like It Is*, is now one of the highest-ranking shows on Manhattan cable. Of course, it's public access so it's not like she's making any money off it, but a bunch of the major networks picked up this interview she did of me one night when I was half asleep and played it. I thought it was stupid, but I guess a lot of other people thought it was good because now Lilly gets tons of viewer mail, whereas before the only mail she got was from her stalker, Norman.

Michael: Look, if you're having time management issues, don't take it out on me. Just don't expect me to meekly do your bidding, especially when you already owe me one.

Me: Lilly, no offence, but I don't think this week's a good time for a walkout, anyway. I mean, after all, it's almost Finals.

Lilly: SO???

Me: So some of us really need to stay in class. I can't afford to miss any review sessions. I'm getting bad enough grades as it is.

Michael: Really? I thought you were doing better in Algebra.

Me: If you call a D plus better.

Michael: Aw, come on. You have to be making better than a D plus. Your mom is married to your Algebra teacher!

Me: So? That doesn't mean anything. You know Mr G doesn't play favourites.

Michael: I would think he'd cut his own stepdaughter a little slack, is all.

Lilly: WOULD YOU TWO PLEASE PAY ATTENTION TO THE SITUATION AT HAND, WHICH IS THE FACT THAT

THIS SCHOOL IS IN VITAL NEED OF
SERIOUS REFORM?

Fortunately, at that moment the bell rang, so no walkout tomorrow as far as I know. Which is a good thing, because I really need the extra study time.

You know, it's funny about Mrs Spears not liking Lilly's term paper proposal, because she was very enthusiastic about my proposal, *A Case Against Christmas Trees: Why We Must Curtail the Pagan Ritual of Chopping Down Pine Trees Every December if We Are Going to Repair the Ozone Layer.*

And my IQ isn't anywhere near as high as Lilly's.

Monday, December 7, Bio.

Kenny just passed me the following note:

> *Mia – I hope what I said to you last night didn't make you feel uncomfortable. I just wanted you to know how I felt.*
>
> > *Sincerely,*
> > *Kenny*

Oh, God. Now what am I supposed to do? He's sitting here next to me, waiting for an answer. In fact, that's what he thinks I'm writing right now. An answer.

What do I say?

Maybe this is my perfect opportunity to break up with him. *I'm sorry, Kenny, but I don't feel the same way – let's just be friends.* Is that what I should say?

It's just that I don't want to hurt his feelings, you know? And he is my Bio. partner. I mean, whatever happens, I am going to have to sit by him for the next two weeks. And I would much rather have a Bio. partner who likes me than one who hates me.

And what about the dance? I mean, if I break up with him, who am I going to go to the Non-Denominational Winter Dance with? I know it is horrible to think things like this, but this is the first dance in the history of my life to which I already have a date.

Well, I mean, if he'd ever get around to asking me, anyway.

And how about that Final, huh? Our Bio. Final, I mean. No way am I going to be able to pass without Kenny's notes. NO WAY.

But what else can I do? I mean, considering what happened today at the salad bar.

This is it. Goodbye, date for the Non-Denominational Winter Dance. Hello, Saturday night television.

Dear Kenny,

It isn't that I don't think of you as a very dear friend. It's just that—

Monday, December 7, 3 p.m., Mr Gianini's Algebra Review

OK, so the bell rang before I had time to finish my note.

That doesn't mean I'm not going to tell Kenny exactly how I feel. I totally am. Tonight, as a matter of fact. I don't care if it's cruel to do something like that over the phone. I just can't take it any more.

Homework:

Algebra: review questions at the end of Chapters 1–3
English: term paper
World Civ.: review questions at the end of Chapters 1–4
G & T: none
French: review questions at the end of Chapters 1–3
Biology: review questions at the end of Chapters 1–5

Tuesday, December 8, Homeroom

All right. So I didn't break up with him.

I totally meant to.

And it wasn't even because I didn't have the heart to do it over the phone, either.

It was something GRANDMERE, of all people, said.

Not that I feel right about it. Not breaking up with him, I mean. It's just that after Algebra review I had to go to the showroom where Sebastiano is flogging his latest creations, so that he could have his flunkies take my measurements for my dress. Grandmere was going on about how from now on, I should really only wear clothes by Genovian designers, to show my patriotism or whatever. Which is going to be hard, because, uh, there's only one Genovian clothing designer that I know of and that's Sebastiano. And let's just say he doesn't make very much out of denim.

But whatever. I so had more important things to worry about than my spring wardrobe.

Which I guess Grandmere must have caught on to, because midway through Sebastiano's description of the beading he was going to have sewn on to my gown's bodice, Grandmere slammed down her Sidecar and shouted, 'Amelia, what is the matter with you?'

I must have jumped about a foot in the air. 'What?'

'Sebastiano asked if you prefer a sweetheart or square-cut neckline.'

I stared at her blankly. 'Neckline for what?'

Grandmere gave me the Evil Eye. She does this quite frequently. That's why my father, even though he has the neighbouring hotel suite, never stops by during my princess lessons.

'Sebastiano,' my grandmother said. 'You will please leave the princess and myself for a moment.'

And Sebastiano – who was wearing a new pair of leather trousers, these in a tangerine colour (the new grey, he told me. And white, you might be surprised to know, is the new black.) – bowed and left the room, followed by the slinky ladies who'd been taking my measurements.

'Now,' Grandmere said, imperiously. 'Something is clearly troubling you, Amelia. What is it?'

'It's nothing,' I said, turning all red. I knew I was turning all red because a) I could feel it, and b) I could see my reflection in the three full-length mirrors in front of me.

'It is not nothing.' Grandmere took in a healthy drag from her Gitanes, even though I have asked her repeatedly not to smoke in my presence since breathing second-hand smoke can cause just as much lung damage as actually smoking. 'What is it? Trouble at home? Your mother and the maths teacher fighting already, I suppose. Well, I never expected *that* marriage to last. Your mother is much too flighty.'

I have to admit, I kind of snapped when she said that. Grandmere is always putting my mother down, even though Mom has raised me pretty much single-handedly and I certainly haven't gotten pregnant or shot anyone yet.

'For your information,' I said, 'my mom and Mr Gianini are blissfully happy together. I wasn't thinking about them at all.'

'What is it, then?' Grandmere asked, in a bored voice.

'Nothing,' I practically yelled. 'I just – well, I was thinking about the fact that I have to break up with my boyfriend tonight, that's all. Not that it's any of your business.'

Instead of taking offence at my tone, which any self-respecting grandparent would have found insolent, Grandmere only took a sip of her drink and suddenly looked way interested.

'Oh?' she said, in a totally different tone of voice – the same tone of voice she uses when someone mentions a stock tip she thinks might be useful for her portfolio. 'What boyfriend is this?'

God, what did I ever do to be cursed with such a grandmother? Seriously. Lilly and Michael's grandma remembers the names of all their friends, makes them rugelach all the time, and always worries that they're not getting enough to eat, even though their parents, the Drs Moscovitz, are wholly reliable at bringing home groceries or at least ordering out.

Me? I get the grandma with the hairless poodle and the nine-carat diamond rings whose greatest joy in life is to torture me.

And why does she enjoy that so much? I've never done anything to her. Nothing except be her only living grandchild, anyway. And it isn't exactly like I go around advertising how I feel about her. You know, I've never actually *told* her I think she's a mean old lady who contributes to the destruction of the environment by wearing fur coats and smoking filterless French cigarettes.

'Grandmere,' I said, trying to remain calm. 'I have only one boyfriend. His name is Kenny.' I've only told you about fifty thousand times, I added, in my head.

'I thought this Kenny person was your Biology partner,' Grandmere said, after taking a sip of her Sidecar.

'He is,' I said, a little surprised that she'd managed to remember something like that. 'He's also my boyfriend. Only the other night he went completely schizo on me and told me he loves me.'

62

Grandmere patted Rommel, who was sitting in her lap looking miserable (his habitual expression), on the head.

'And what is so wrong,' Grandmere wanted to know, 'about a boy who says he loves you?'

'Nothing,' I said. 'Only I'm not in love with him, see? So it wouldn't be fair of me to, you know, lead him on.'

Grandmere raised her painted-on eyebrows. 'I don't see why not.'

How had I ever gotten into this conversation? 'Because, Grandmere. People just don't go around *doing* things like that. Not nowadays.'

'Is that so? Well, I've never observed such a thing. Except, of course, if one happens to be in love with someone else. Then shedding an undesirable suitor might be considered wise, so that one can make oneself available for the man one truly likes.' She eyed me. 'Is there someone like that in your life, Amelia? Someone, ahem, special?'

'No,' I lied, automatically.

Grandmere snorted. 'You're lying.'

'No, I'm not,' I lied.

'Indeed you are. I oughtn't to tell you this, but I suppose as it is a bad habit for a future monarch you ought to be made aware of it, so that in the future you can try to prevent it. When you lie, Amelia, your nostrils flare.'

I threw my hands up to my nose. 'They do not!'

'Indeed,' Grandmere said, clearly enjoying herself immensely. 'If you do not believe me, look in the mirror.'

I turned around to face the nearby full-length mirrors. Taking my hands from my face, I examined my nose. My nostrils weren't flaring. She was crazy.

'I'll ask you again, Amelia,' Grandmere said, in a lazy voice, from her chair. 'Are you in love with anyone right now?'

'No,' I lied automatically . . .

And my nostrils flared right out!

Oh my God! All these years I've been lying and it turns out whenever I do, my nostrils totally give me away!

How could no one have pointed this out to me before? And Grandmere – Grandmere, of all people – was the one who figured it out! Not my mother, with whom I've lived for fourteen years. Not my best friend, whose IQ is higher than Einstein's.

If this got out, my life was over.

'Fine,' I cried dramatically, spinning away from the mirror to face her. 'All right, yes. Yes, I am in love with somebody else. Are you happy now?'

Grandmere raised her painted-on eyebrows.

'No need to shout, Amelia,' she said, with what I might have taken for amusement in anyone other than her. 'Who might this special someone be?'

'Oh, no,' I said, holding out both my hands. If it wouldn't have been totally rude, I'd have made a little cross out of my index fingers and held it up towards her – that's how much she scares me. And if you think about it, with her tattooed eyeliner she does look a little like Nosferatu. 'You are not getting that information out of me.'

Grandmere stubbed out her cigarette in this ashtray Sebastiano had provided, and went, 'Very well. I take it, then, that the gentleman in question does not return your ardour.'

There was no point in lying to her. Not now. Not with my nostrils.

My shoulders sagged. 'No. He likes this other girl. This really smart girl who knows how to clone fruit flies.'

Grandmere snorted. 'A useful talent. Well, never mind

that now. I don't suppose, Amelia, that you are acquainted with the expression "dirty dishwater is better than none"?'

I guess she must have been able to tell from my perplexed expression that this was one I hadn't heard before, since she went on, 'Do not throw away this Kenny until you have managed to secure someone better.'

I stared at her, horrified. Really, my grandmother has said – and done – some pretty cold things in her time, but this one took the biscuit.

'Secure someone better?' I couldn't believe she actually meant what I thought she meant. 'You mean I shouldn't break up with Kenny until I've got someone else?'

Grandmere lit another cigarette. 'But of course.'

'But, Grandmere.' I swear to God, sometimes I can't figure out if she's human or some kind of alien life force sent down from another planet to spy on us. 'You can't do that. You can't just string a guy along like that, knowing that you don't feel the same way about him that he feels about you.'

Grandmere exhaled a long plume of blue smoke. 'Why not?'

'Because it's completely unethical!' I shook my head. 'No. I'm breaking up with Kenny. Right away. Tonight, as a matter of fact.'

Grandmere stroked Rommel under the chin. He looked more miserable than ever, as if instead of stroking him she was peeling the skin away from his body. He really is the most heinous excuse for a dog I have ever seen.

'That,' Grandmere said, 'is your prerogative, of course. But allow me to point out to you that if you break off your relationship with this young man, your Biology grade will suffer.'

I was shocked. But mostly because this was something I

had already thought of myself. I was amazed Grandmere and I had actually shared something.

Which was really the only reason I shouted, 'Grandmere!'

'Well,' Grandmere said, flicking ash from her cigarette into the nearby crystal ashtray. 'Isn't it true? You are only making what, a C, in this class? And that is only because that young man allows you to copy his answers to the homework.'

'Grandmere!' I yelled again. Because, of course, she's right.

She looked at the ceiling. 'Let me see,' she said. 'With your D in Algebra, if you get anything less than a C in Biology your grade point average will take quite a little dip this semester.'

'Grandmere.' I couldn't believe this. She was right. She was so right. But still. 'I am not going to postpone breaking up with Kenny until after the Final. That would be just plain wrong.'

'Suit yourself,' Grandmere said with a sigh. 'But it will certainly be awkward having to sit beside him for the next – how long is it until the end of the semester? – oh, yes, two weeks. Especially considering the fact that after you break things off with him, he probably won't even speak to you any more.'

God, so true. And not something I hadn't thought of myself. If Kenny got mad enough over me breaking up with him not to want to speak to me any more, sixth period was going to be plenty unpleasant.

'And what about this dance?' Grandmere rattled the ice in her Sidecar. 'This Christmas dance?'

'It's not a Christmas dance,' I said. 'It's a non-denominational—'

Grandmere waved a hand. The spiky charm bracelet she was wearing tinkled.

'Whatever,' she said. 'If you stop seeing this young man, who will you go to the dance with?'

'I won't go with anybody,' I said firmly, even though, of course, my heart was breaking at the thought. 'I'll just stay home.'

'While everyone else has a good time? Really, Amelia, you aren't being at all sensible. What about this other young man?'

'What other young man?'

'The one you claim to be so in love with. Won't he be at this dance with the house fly girl?'

'Fruit fly,' I corrected her. 'And I don't know. Maybe.'

The thought that Michael might ask Judith Gershner to the Non-Denominational Winter Dance had never occurred to me. But as soon as Grandmere mentioned it, I felt that same sickening sensation I'd felt at the ice-skating rink when I'd first seen them together: kind of like the time when Lilly and I were crossing Bleecker Street and this Chinese food delivery man crashed into us on his bicycle and I had all the wind knocked out of me.

Only this time it wasn't just my chest that hurt, but my tongue. It had been feeling a lot better but now it started to throb again.

'It seems to me,' Grandmere said, 'that one way to get this young man's attention might be to show up at the dance on the arm of this other young man, looking perfectly divine in an original creation by Genovian fashion designer, Sebastiano Grimaldi.'

I just stared at her. Because she was right. She was so right. Except . . .

'Grandmere,' I said. 'The guy I like? Well, he likes girls

who can *clone insects*. OK? I highly doubt he is going to be impressed by a *dress*.'

I didn't mention that I had, of course, just the other night, been hoping that very thing.

But almost as if she could read my mind, Grandmere just went, 'Hmm,' in this knowing way.

'Suit yourself,' she continued. 'Still, it seems a bit cruel to me, your breaking things off with this young man at this time of year.'

'Why?' I asked, confused. Had Grandmere inadvertently stumbled across some TV channel playing *It's a Wonderful Life* or something? She had never shown one speck of holiday spirit before now. 'Because it's *Christmas*?'

'No,' Grandmere said, looking very disgusted with me – I guess over the suggestion that she might ever be moved by the anniversary of the birth of anyone's saviour. 'Because of your exams. If you truly wish to be kind, I think you might at least wait until your Final exams are over before breaking the poor little fellow's heart.'

I had been all ready to argue with whatever excuse for me not breaking up with Kenny Grandmere came up with next – but this one I had not expected. I stood there with my mouth hanging open. I know it was hanging open, because I could see it reflected in the three full-length mirrors beside me.

'I cannot imagine,' Grandmere went on, 'why you do not simply allow him to believe his ardour returned until your exams are over. Why compound the poor boy's stress? But you must, of course, do what you think is best. I suppose this, er, Kenny is the sort of boy who bounces back easily from rejection? He'll probably do quite well in his exams, in spite of his broken heart.'

Oh, God! If she had stabbed a fork in my stomach and

twisted my intestines around the tines like spaghetti noodles, she couldn't have made me feel worse . . .

And, I have to admit, a little relieved. Because of course I can't break up with Kenny now. Never mind my Bio. grade and the dance – you can't break up with someone right before Finals. It's like the meanest thing you can do.

Well, aside from the kind of stuff Lana and her friends pull. You know, girls' locker room stuff, like going up to someone who is changing and asking her why she wears a bra when she obviously doesn't need one, or making fun of her just because she doesn't happen to like being kissed by her boyfriend. That kind of thing.

So here I am. I *want* to break up with Kenny, but I can't.

I *want* to tell Michael how I feel about him, but I can't do that either.

I can't even quit biting my fingernails. I am going to gross out an entire European nation with my bleedy-looking cuticles.

I am a pathetic mess. No wonder in the car this morning – after I accidentally closed the door on Lars's foot – Lilly said that I should really look into getting some therapy, because if anybody needs to discover harmony between her conscious and her unconscious, it's me.

To Do Before Leaving for Genovia

1. Get cat food, litter for Fat Louie.
2. Stop biting fingernails.
3. Achieve self-actualization.
4. Discover harmony between conscious and subconscious.
5. Break up with Kenny – but not until after Finals/Non-Denominational Winter Dance.

Tuesday, December 8, English

What was THAT just now in the hallway? Did Kenny Showalter just say what I think he said to you?

Yes. Oh my God, Shameeka, what am I going to do? I'm shaking so hard I can barely write – M

What do you mean, what are you going to do? The boy is warm for your form, Mia. Go for it.

People can't just be allowed to go around saying things like that. Especially so loud. Everyone must have heard him. Do you think everyone heard him?

Everybody heard him, all right. You should have seen Lilly's face. I thought she was going to suffer one of those synaptic breakdowns she's always talking about.

You think EVERYBODY heard him? I mean, like the people coming out of the Chemistry lab? Do you think they heard?

How could they not? He yelled it pretty loud.

Were they laughing? The people coming out of Chemistry? They weren't laughing, were they?

Most of them were laughing.

Oh, God! Why was I ever born????

Except Michael. He wasn't laughing.

He WASN'T? REALLY? Are you pulling my leg?

No. Why would I do that? And what do you care what Michael Moscovitz thinks, anyway?

I don't. I don't care. What makes you think I care?

Um, for one thing because you won't shut up about it.

People shouldn't go around laughing at other people's misfortunes. That's all.

I don't see what the big misfortune is. So the guy loves you? A lot of girls would really like it if their boyfriend yelled that at them between second and third period.

Yeah, well, NOT ME!!!!

Use **transitive verbs** to create brief, vigorous sentences:
   Transitive: He soon regretted his words.
   Intransitive: It was not long before he was very sorry that he had said what he said.

Tuesday, December 8, Bio.

Gifted and Talented was so not fun today. Not that Bio. is any better, on account of the fact that I am stuck here next to Kenny, who seems to have calmed down a little since this morning.

Still, I really think that people who are not actually enrolled in certain classes have no business showing up in them.

For instance, just because Judith Gershner has study hall for fifth period is no reason that she should be allowed to hang around the Gifted and Talented classroom for fifty minutes during that period. She should never have been let out of study hall in the first place. I don't think she even had a pass.

Not that I would turn her in, or anything. But this kind of flagrant rule-breaking really shouldn't be encouraged. If Lilly is going to go through with this walkout thing, which she is still trying to garner support for, she should really add to her list of complaints the fact that the teachers in this school have favourites. I mean, just because a girl knows how to clone things doesn't mean she should be allowed to roam the school freely any time she wants.

But there she was when I walked in, and there's no doubt about it: Judith Gershner has a total crush on Michael. I don't really know how he feels about her, but she was wearing tan-coloured pantyhose instead of the black cotton tights she normally wears, so you *know* something is up. No girl wears tan pantyhose without a good reason.

And, OK, so maybe they are working on their booth for the Winter Carnival, but that is no reason for Judith to drape her arm across the back of Michael's chair like that. Plus he used to help me with my Algebra homework during G & T, but now he can't because Judith is monopolizing all his time. I would think he might resent the intrusion.

Plus Judith really has no business butting into my private conversations. She hardly even knows me.

But did that stop her from observing, when she overheard Lilly's formal apology for not having believed me about Kenny's weird phone call – any doubts about the veracity of which he managed to scatter today with his display of unbridled passion in the third-floor hallway – that she feels sorry for him? Oh, no.

'Poor kid,' Judith said. 'I heard what he said to you in the hallway. I was in the Chem. lab. What was it again? "I don't care if you don't feel the same way, Mia, I will always love you", or something like that?'

I didn't say anything. That's because I was busy picturing how Judith would look with a pencil sticking out of the middle of her forehead.

'It's really sweet,' Judith said. 'If you think about it. I mean, the guy's clearly got it bad for you.'

This is the problem, see. Everyone thinks that what Kenny did was so cute and everything. Nobody seems to understand that it wasn't cute. It wasn't cute at all. It was completely humiliating. I don't think I've ever been so embarrassed in my whole life.

And, believe me, I've lived through more than my fair share of embarrassing incidents, especially since this whole princess thing started.

But I'm apparently the only person in this entire school who thinks what Kenny did was the least bit wrong.

'He's obviously very in touch with his emotions.' Even Lilly was taking Kenny's side in the whole thing. 'Unlike *some* people.'

I have to say, this makes me so mad when I think about it because, the truth is, ever since I have started writing things down in journals, I have gotten very in touch with my emotions. I usually know almost exactly how I feel.

The problem is, I just can't tell anyone.

I don't know who was the most surprised when Michael suddenly came to my defence against his sister – Lilly, Judith Gershner, or me.

'Just because Mia doesn't go around shouting about how she feels in the third-floor hallway,' Michael said, 'doesn't mean she isn't in touch with her emotions.'

How does he do that? How is it that he is able to magically put into words exactly what I feel but seem to have so much trouble saying? This, you see, is why I love him. I mean, how could I not?

'Yeah,' I said triumphantly, to Lilly.

'Well, you could have said something back to him.' Lilly always gets disgruntled when Michael comes to my rescue – especially when he does it while she is attacking me about the lack of honesty in my emotional life. 'Instead of just leaving him hanging there.'

'And what,' I demanded – injudiciously, I now realize – 'should I have said to him?'

'How about,' Lilly said, 'that you love him back?'

WHY? That's all I want to know. WHY was I cursed with a best friend who doesn't understand that there are some things you just don't say in front of EVERYONE IN THE ENTIRE GIFTED AND TALENTED CLASS-ROOM, INCLUDING HER BROTHER????

The problem is, Lilly has never been embarrassed about anything in her life. She simply does not know the meaning of the word embarrassment.

'Look,' I said, feeling my cheeks begin to burn. I couldn't lie, of course. How could I lie, considering what I now know about my nostrils? OK, Lilly hadn't figured it out yet, but it was only a matter of time.

'I really and truly value Kenny's companionship,' I said carefully. 'But love. I mean, *love*. That is a very big thing. I'm not, I mean, I don't . . . '

I dribbled off pathetically, acutely aware that everyone in the room, but most especially Michael, was listening.

'I see,' Lilly said, narrowing her eyes. 'Fear of commitment.'

'I do not fear commitment,' I insisted. 'I just—'

But Lilly's dark eyes were already shining in eager anticipation. She was getting ready to psychoanalyze me – one of her favourite hobbies, unfortunately.

'Let's examine the situation, shall we?' she said. 'I mean, here you've got this guy going around the hallways screaming about how much he loves you, and you just stare at him like a rat caught in the path of the D train. What do you suppose that means?'

'Have you ever considered,' I demanded, 'that maybe the reason I didn't tell him I love him back is because I—'

I almost said it. Really. I did. I almost said that I don't love Kenny.

But I couldn't. Because if I'd said that, somehow it would have gotten back to Kenny and that would be even worse than my breaking up with him. I couldn't do it.

So all I said instead was, 'Lilly, you know perfectly well I do not fear commitment. I mean, there are lots boys I—'

'Oh, yeah?' Lilly seemed to be enjoying herself way more

76

than usual. It was almost as if she was playing to an audience. Which, of course, she was. The audience of her brother and his girlfriend. 'Name one.'

'One what?'

'Name a boy that you could see yourself committing to for all eternity.'

'What do you want – a list?' I asked her.

'A list would be nice,' Lilly said.

So I drew up the following list:

Guys Mia Thermopolis Could See Herself Committing To for All Eternity

1. Wolverine of the *X-men*.
2. That Gladiator guy.
3. Will Smith.
4. Tarzan from the Disney cartoon.
5. The Beast from *Beauty and the Beast*.
6. That hot soldier guy from *Mulan*.
7. The guy Brendan Fraser played in *The Mummy*.
8. Angel.
9. Tom on *Daria*.
10. Justin Baxendale.

But this list turned out to be no good, because Lilly totally took it and analyzed it, and it works out that half the guys on it are actually cartoon characters; one is a vampire, and one is a mutant who can make spikes shoot out of his knuckles.

In fact, except for Will Smith and Justin Baxendale – the good-looking senior who just transferred from Trinity and who a lot of girls at Albert Einstein High School are already in love with – all the guys I listed are fictional creations. Apparently, the fact that I could list no guy I had a hope of actually getting together with – or who even lives in the third dimension – is indicative of something.

Not, of course, indicative of the fact that the guy I like was actually in the room at the time, sitting next to his new girlfriend, and so I couldn't list him.

Oh, no. Nobody thought of *that*.

No, the lack of actual attainable men on my list was apparently indicative of my unrealistic expectations where men are concerned, and further proof of my inability to commit.

Lilly says if I don't lower my expectations somewhat I am destined for an unsatisfactory love life.

As if the way things have been going, I've ever expected anything else.

Kenny just tossed me this note:

Mia – I'm sorry about what happened today in the hallway. I understand now that I embarrassed you. Sometimes I forget that even though you are a princess, you are still quite introverted. I promise never to do anything of the sort again. Can I make it up to you by taking you to lunch at Big Wong on Thursday? – Kenny

I said yes, of course. Not just because I really like Big Wong's steamed vegetable dumplings, or even because I don't want people thinking I fear commitment. I didn't even say yes because I suspect that, over dumplings and hot tea, Kenny is finally going to ask me to the Non-Denominational Winter Dance.

I said yes because, in spite of it all, I really do like Kenny, and I don't want to hurt his feelings.

And I'd feel the same way even if I weren't a princess and always had to do the right thing.

Homework:

Algebra: review questions at the end of Chapters 4–7
English: term paper
World Civ.: review questions at the end of Chapters 5–9
G & T: none
French: review questions at the end of Chapters 4–6
Biology: review questions at the end of Chapters 6–8

Tuesday, December 8, 4 p.m., in the Limo on the Way to the Plaza

The following conversation took place between Mr Gianini and me today after Algebra review:

Mr G: Mia, is everything all right?

Me: (*Surprised*) Yes. Why wouldn't it be?

Mr G: Well, it's just that I thought you'd pretty much grasped the FOIL method, but on today's pop quiz you got all five problems wrong.

Me: I guess I've sort of had a lot on my mind.

Mr G: Your trip to Genovia?

Me: Yeah, that, and . . . other things.

Mr G: Well, if you want to talk about the, um, other things, you know I'm always here for you. And your mother. I know we might seem preoccupied with the baby and everything, but you're always number one on our list of priorities. You know that, don't you?

Me: (*Mortified*) Yes. But there's nothing wrong. Really.

Thank God he doesn't know about my nostrils.

And, really, what else *could* I have said? 'Mr G, my boyfriend is a nutcase but I can't break up with him on account of Finals, and I'm in love with my best friend's brother?'

I highly doubt he'd be able to offer any meaningful advice on any of the above.

Tuesday, December 8, 7 p.m.

I don't believe this. I'm home before *Baywatch Hawaii* starts for the first time in like months. Something must be wrong with Grandmere. Although she seemed pretty normal at our lesson today. I mean, for her. Except that she kept stopping me in the middle of my reciting the Genovian pledge of allegiance (which I have to memorize, of course, for when I am visiting schools in Genovia. I don't want to look like an idiot in front of a bunch of five-year-olds for not knowing it) to ask me what I'd decided to do about Kenny.

It's kind of funny about her taking an interest in my personal life since she certainly never has before. Well, not very much, anyway.

And she kept on saying stuff about how ingenious it had been of Kenny, sending me those anonymous love letters last October – the ones I thought (well, OK, *hoped*, not really thought) Michael was writing.

I was all, 'What was so ingenious about *that*?' to which Grandmere just replied, 'Well, you're his girlfriend now, aren't you?'

Which I never really thought about, but I guess she's right.

Anyway, my mom was so surprised to see me home so early she actually let me be in charge of choosing the take-out (pizza margherita for me. I let her get rigatoni bolognese, even though the sausage in the sauce is probably steeped in nitrates that could harm a developing foetus. Still, it was sort of a special occasion, what with me actually being home for dinner for a change. Even Mr Gianini got a little wild and had something with porcini mushrooms in it).

I am psyched to be home early because you wouldn't believe all the studying I have to do, plus I should probably start my term paper, then there's figuring out what I'm going to get people for Christmas and Hanukkah, not to mention going over the thank you speech I have to make to the people of Genovia in my nationally televised (in Genovia, anyway) introduction to the people I will one day rule.

I had really better buckle down and get to work!

Tuesday, December 8, 7:30 p.m.

OK, so I was taking a study break and I just realized something. You can learn *a lot* from watching *Baywatch*. Seriously.
  I have complied a list:

Things I Have Learned from Watching *Baywatch*

1. If you are paralyzed from the waist down, you just need to see a kid being attacked by a murderer and you will be able to get up and save him.
2. If you have bulimia, it is probably because two men love you at the same time. Just tell the two of them you only want to be friends and your bulimia will go away.
3. It is always easy to get a parking place near the beach.
4. Male lifeguards always put a shirt on when they leave the beach. Female lifeguards don't need to bother.
5. If you meet a beautiful but troubled girl, she is probably either a diamond smuggler or suffering from a split personality disorder. Do not accept her invitation to dinner.
6. Dick van Patten, though a senior citizen, can be surprisingly hard to quell in a fistfight.
7. If people are dying mysteriously in the water, it is probably because a giant electric eel has escaped from a nearby aquarium.
8. Girls who are thinking about abandoning their baby should just leave it on the beach. Chances are, a nice lifeguard will take it home, adopt it, and raise it as his own.
9. It is very easy to outswim a shark.
10. Wild seals make adorable and easily trained pets.

Tuesday, December 8, 8:30 p.m.

I just got an e-mail from Lilly. I'm not the only one who got it, either. Somehow she figured out how to do a mass e-mail to every kid in school.

Well, I shouldn't be surprised, I guess. She *is* a genius. Still, she has clearly developed atrophy of the brain from too much studying, because look what she wrote:

```
         Attention all students at
         Albert Einstein High School


Stressed from too many exams, term papers and
final projects? Don't just passively accept the
oppressive workload handed down to us by the
tyrannical administration! A silent walkout has
been scheduled for tomorrow. At 10 a.m.
exactly, join your fellow students in showing
our teachers how we feel about inflexible exam
schedules, repressive censorship, and having
only one Reading Day in which to prepare for
our Finals. Leave your pencils, leave your
books and gather on East 75th Street between
Madison and Park (use doors by main
administration offices, if possible) for a rally
against Principal Gupta and the trustees. Let
your voice be heard!
```

I am so sure, I can't walk out tomorrow at 10 a.m. That's right in the middle of Algebra. Mr Gianini's feelings will be so hurt if we all just get up and leave.

But if I say I'm not going to take part in it, Lilly will be furious.

But if I do take part in it, my dad will kill me. Not to

84

mention my mom. I mean, we could all get suspended or something. Or hit by a delivery truck. There are a lot of them on 75th at that time of day.

Why? Why must I be saddled with a best friend who is so clearly a sociopath?

Tuesday, December 8, 8:45 p.m.

I just got the following Instant Message from Michael:

```
CracKing: Did you just get that whacked-out
mass e-mail from my sister?
```

I replied at once.

```
FtLouie: Yes.
>
CracKing: You're not going along with her
stupid walkout, are you?
>
FtLouie: Oh, right. She won't be too mad if I
don't, or anything.
>
CracKing: You don't have to do everything she
says, you know, Mia. I mean, you've stood up
to her before. Why not now?
```

Um, because I have enough to worry about right now –
for instance, Finals; my impending trip to Genovia; and, oh,
yeah, the fact that I love you – without adding a fight with
my best friend to the list.

But I didn't say that, of course.

```
FtLouie: I find that the path of least
resistance is often the safest one when dealing
with your sister.
>
CracKing: Well, I'm not doing it. Walking out,
I mean.
```

>

FtLouie: It's different for you. You're her
brother. She has to remain on speaking terms
with you. You live together.
>

CracKing: Not for much longer. Thank God.

Oh, right. He's going away to college soon.
Well, not too far away. About a hundred blocks or so.

FtLouie: That's right. You got accepted to
Columbia. Early decision too. I never did
congratulate you. So, congratulations.
>

CracKing: Thanks.
>

FtLouie: You must be happy that you'll know at
least one other person there. Judith Gershner,
I mean.
>

CracKing: Yeah, I guess so. Listen, you're
still going to be in town for the Winter
Carnival, right? I mean, you're not leaving for
Genovia before the 18th, are you?

All I could think was, *Why is he asking me this? I mean, he can't
be going to ask me to the dance. He must know I'm going with Kenny.
I mean, if Kenny ever gets around to asking me, that is. Besides, it isn't
as if Michael is available. Isn't he going with Judith? Well? ISN'T
HE?*

FtLouie: I'm leaving for Genovia on the 19th.
>

CracKing: Oh, good. Because you should really stop by the Computer Club's booth at the Carnival and check out this program I've been working on. I think you'll like it.

I should have known. Michael isn't going to ask me to any dance. Not in this lifetime, anyway. I should have known it was just his stupid computer program he wanted me to see. Who even cares? I suppose dumb Army guys will pop out at me, and I'll have to shoot them or whatever. Judith's idea, I'm sure.

I wanted to write to him, *Don't you have the slightest idea what I'm going through? That the only person whom I can see myself committing to for all eternity is YOU? Don't you KNOW that by now????*

But instead I wrote:

FtLouie: Can't wait. Well, I have to go. Bye.

Sometimes I completely hate myself.

Wednesday, December 9, 3 a.m.

You're never going to believe this. Something *Grandmere* said is keeping me awake.

Seriously. I was dead asleep – well, as asleep as you can be with a twenty-five-pound cat purring on your abdomen – when all of a sudden I woke up with this totally random phrase going around in my head:

'Well, you're his girlfriend now, aren't you?'

That's what Grandmere said when I asked her what was so ingenious about Kenny having sent me those anonymous love letters.

And do you know what?

SHE'S RIGHT.

It seems totally bizarre to admit that Grandmere might be right about something, but I think it's true. Kenny's anonymous love letters DID work. I mean, I AM his girlfriend now.

So what's to keep me from writing some anonymous love letters to the boy *I* like? I mean, really? Besides the fact that I already have a boyfriend, and the guy I like already has a girlfriend?

I think this is a plan that might have some merit. It needs further work, of course, but hey, desperate measures call for desperate times. Or something like that. Too sleepy to figure it out.

Wednesday, December 9, Homeroom

OK, I was up all night thinking about it, and I'm pretty sure I've got it figured out. Even as I sit here, my plan is being put into action, thanks to Tina Hakim Baba and a stop at Ho's Deli before school started.

Actually, Ho's didn't really have what I wanted. I wanted a card that was blank inside, with a picture on the front that was sophisticated but not too sexy. But the only blank cards they had at Ho's (that weren't plastered with drawings of kittens on them) were ones with photos of fruit being dipped into chocolate sauce.

I tried to choose a non-phallic fruit, but even the strawberry I got is kind of sexier than I would have liked. I don't know what's sexy about fruit with chocolate sauce dripping off it, but Tina was like, *Whoa*, when she saw it.

Still, she gamely agreed to print my poem on the inside of the card, so Michael won't recognize my handwriting. She even liked my poem, which I came up with at five this morning:

> *Roses are red*
> *Violets are blue*
> *You may not know it*
> *But someone loves you.*

Not my best work, I will admit, but it was really hard to come up with something better after only three hours of sleep last night.

I hesitated somewhat over the use of the L word. I thought maybe I should substitute Like for Love. I don't want him to think there's a creepy stalker after him, and all.

But Tina said Love was absolutely right. Because, as she put it, 'It's the truth, isn't it?'

And since it's anonymous, I guess it doesn't matter that I am laying open my soul.

Anyway, Tina goes by Michael's locker right before we have PE, so she's going to slip it to him then.

I can't believe that this is the low I have stooped to. But like Dad said, faint heart never won fair lady.

Wednesday, December 9, Later in Homeroom

Lars just pointed out that I'm not exactly risking anything, seeing as how I didn't sign the card and even went to the extreme of having someone else write out the poem for me (Lars knows all about this, on account of the fact I had to explain to him why we had to go into Ho's at eight-fifteen in the morning). He helped pick the card, but I would be happy if that was the extent of his contribution to this particular project. As a man, I cannot imagine his input is at all valuable.

Besides, he's been married like four times, so I highly doubt he knows anything about romance.

Also, he should know by now we're not allowed to talk during homeroom.

Wednesday, December 9, Algebra, 9:30 a.m.

I just saw Lilly in the hallway. She whispered, 'DON'T FORGET! TEN O'CLOCK! DON'T LET ME DOWN!'

Well, the truth is, I did forget. The walkout! The stupid walkout!

And poor Mr Gianini, standing up there going over Chapter Five, not suspecting a thing. It's not his fault Mrs Spears didn't like Lilly's term paper topic. Lilly can't just arbitrarily punish all the teachers in school for something one teacher did.

It's already nine thirty-five. What am I going to do?

Lana just leaned back and hissed, 'You gonna walk out with your fat friend?'

I take real objection to this. Only in a culture as screwed up as ours, where girls like Christina Aguilera are held up as models of beauty, when clearly they are in fact suffering from some sort of malnutrition (scurvy?), would Lilly ever be considered fat. Because Lilly isn't fat. She is just round, like a puppy.

I hate it here.

Wednesday, December 9, Algebra, 9:50 a.m.

Ten minutes until the walkout. I can't take this. I'm getting out.

OK. I'm standing in the hallway next to the fire alarm by the second-floor drinking fountain. I got a hall pass from Mr G. I told him I had to go to the bathroom.

Lars is with me, of course. I wish he'd stop laughing. He does not seem to realize the seriousness of the situation. Plus Justin Baxendale just walked by with a hall pass of his own, and he gave us this really weird look.

Yeah, I probably do look a little strange, hanging out in the hallway with my bodyguard, who is currently experiencing a fit of the giggles, but still. I do not need to be looked at weirdly by Justin Baxendale.

His eyelashes are really long and dark and they make his eyes look sort of smoky . . .

OH MY GOD! I CAN'T BELIEVE I AM WRITING ABOUT JUSTIN BAXENDALE'S EYELASHES AT A TIME LIKE THIS!

I mean, I am in a real bind here:

If I do not walk out with Lilly, I'll lose my best friend.

But if I do walk out with everyone, I will be totally dissing my stepfather.

So I really only have one choice.

Lars just offered to do it for me. But I can't let him. I can't let him take the fall for me if we get caught. I am the princess. I have to do it myself.

I just told him to get ready to run. This is one time being so tall comes in handy. I have a pretty long stride.

Well, here goes.

Wednesday, December 9, 10 a.m., East 75th Street, Beneath Some Scaffolding

I don't get why she's so mad. I mean, yeah, it isn't the same thing if everyone evacuates the building due to a fire alarm going off as opposed to everyone leaving in protest against the repressive teaching techniques of some of the teachers.

But we're still all standing in the middle of the street in the rain, and nobody has coats on because they wouldn't let us stop at our lockers for fear we'd all be consumed in a fiery conflagration, so we're probably going to get hypothermia from the cold and die.

That's what she wanted, right?

But no. She can't even be happy about that.

'Somebody ratted us out!' she keeps yelling. 'Somebody told! Why else would they schedule a fire drill for exactly the same time as my walkout? I'm telling you, these bureaucrats will stop at nothing to keep us from speaking out against them. Nothing! They'll even make us stand out in freezing drizzle, hoping to weaken our immune systems so we'll no longer have the strength to fight them. Well, I, for one, refuse to catch cold! I refuse to succumb to their petty abuses!'

I suggested to Lilly that she write her term paper on the suffragettes, because they, like us, had to put up with numerous indignities in their battle for equal rights.

Lilly, however, told me not to be facile.

God, being best friends with a genius is hard.

97

Wednesday, December 9, Gifted and Talented

I can't tell if Michael got the card or not!!!!

Worse, stupid Judith Gershner is here AGAIN. Why can't she stay in her own class? Why is she always hanging around ours? We were all getting along perfectly well until SHE came along.

My life is pathetic.

I thought about going across the hall to the teachers' lounge and asking Mrs Hill a question about something – like why she had the custodians remove the door to the supply closet so we can't lock Boris in there any more – so she'd maybe look over and NOTICE that there's a girl in our classroom who is NOT supposed to be there.

But I couldn't bring myself to do it, because of Michael. I mean, Michael obviously WANTS Judith here or else he'd tell her to go away.

RIGHT?????

Anyway, with Michael so busy and all with Miss Gershner, I guess I am on my own with the whole Algebra review thing.

That's all right. I'm completely fine with that. I can study on my own just fine. Watch:

A, B, C = disjoint partition of universal set
Collection of non-empty subsets of U which are pairwise disjoint and whose union is equal to the set of U

I get that. I totally get what that means. Who needs Michael's help? Not me. I am totally cool with the collection of non-empty subsets.

TOTALLY COOL WITH IT.

Oh, Michael
You have made my heart
a disjoint partition.

Why can't you see
that we were meant to be
a universal set?

Instead, you have turned my soul
into a collection
of non-empty subsets.

I cannot believe
that our love was meant to be
pairwise disjoint.

But rather
a union
equal to the set of
U and me.

Wednesday, December 9, French

You know what else I just realized? That if this thing works – you know, if I do manage to get Michael away from Judith Gershner, and I break up with Kenny, and I end up, you know, in a potentially romantic situation with Lilly's brother – I will not know what to do.

Seriously.

Take kissing, for instance. I have only ever kissed one person before, and that's Kenny. I cannot believe that what Kenny and I did really encompassed the whole of the kissing experience, because it certainly wasn't as fun as people always make it look on TV.

This is a very disturbing thought and has led me to an equally disturbing conclusion: I know very little about kissing.

In fact, it seems to me that if I am going to be doing any kissing with anybody, I should get some advice beforehand. From a kissing expert, I mean.

Which is why I am consulting Tina Hakim Baba. She may not be allowed to wear make-up to school, but she has been kissing Dave Farouq El-Abar – who goes to Trinity – for close to three months now, AND liking it, so I consider her an expert on the subject.

I am enclosing the results of this highly scientific document for future reference:

Tina — I need to know about kissing. Can you please answer each of the following questions IN DETAIL????

And DO NOT show this to anyone!!!! DO NOT lose this paper!!!! — Mia

1. *Can a boy tell if the person he is with is inexperienced? How does an inexperienced kisser kiss (so I can avoid that)?*

Mia — the moment you have been waiting for:
The guy may sense a feeling of nervousness coming from you, or that you are uneasy, but everyone is nervous when they are kissing someone new. It's natural! But kissing is easy to catch on to — believe me! An inexperienced kisser might break away too soon because he or she is scared or whatever. But that is normal. It's weird, kissing someone for the first time. It's SUPPOSED to be weird. That's what makes it fun.

2. *Is there such a thing as a great kisser? If so, what are the qualifications? (So I know what to practise.)*

Yes, there is such a thing as a good kisser. A good kisser is always affectionate and gentle and patient and not demanding.

3. *How much pressure do you exert on his lips? I mean, do you push or, like in a handshake, are you just supposed to be firm? Or are you just supposed to stand there and let him do all the work?*

If you want a gentle kiss (a caring one) don't apply too much pressure (this is also true if he is wearing braces — you don't want to cause any lacerations). If you give a guy a 'harsh' kiss (too much pressure), he might think you are desperate or that you want to go further than you probably do.
Of course you aren't supposed to just stand there and let him do all

the work: kiss him back! But always kiss him the way YOU want to
be kissed. That is how guys learn. If we didn't show them how to do
everything, we'd never get anywhere!

4.   *How do you know when it's time to stop?*

Stop when he stops, or when you feel like you've had enough, or
don't want to go any further. Simply and gently (so you don't freak
him out) move your head back or if the moment is right, you can
change the kiss into a hug then step back.

5.   *If you are in love with him is it still gross?*

Of course not! Kissing is never gross!
Well, OK, I guess I could see that maybe with Kenny, it might be. It
is always better with someone you actually like.
Of course, even with someone you really like, sometimes kissing can
be gross. Once Dave licked me on the chin, and I was all, get away.
But I think that was by accident (the licking).

6.   *If he is in love with you, does he even care if you are bad? (Define*
     bad kisser. See above.)

If the guy likes/loves you, he won't care if you are a good kisser or
not. In fact, even if you are a bad kisser, he will probably think you
are a good one. And vice-versa. He should like you for what you are
— not how you kiss.
DEFINITION OF BAD KISSER: A bad kisser is someone who gets
your face all wet, slobbers on you, sticks his tongue in when you're
not ready, has bad breath, OR sometimes there can be kissers
whose tongues are all dry and prickly like a cactus but I have never
experienced one of those, just heard about them.

7. *When do you know if it's time to open your mouth (thus turning it into a French)?*

You will probably feel his tongue touch your lips. If you want to pursue the idea, open your lips a little. If not, keep them closed. Coming demain — Chapter II: How to French!!!!

Homework:

Algebra: review questions at the end of Chapters 8–10
English: English Journal: Books I Have Read
World Civ.: review questions at the end of Chapters 10–12
G & T: none
French: review questions at the end of Chapters 7–9
Biology: review questions at the end of Chapters 9–12

Wednesday, December 9, 9 p.m., in the Limo Home from Grandmere's

I am so tired I can hardly write. Grandmere made me try on every single dress in Sebastiano's showroom. You wouldn't believe the number of dresses I've had on today. Short ones, long ones, straight-skirted ones and poofy-skirted ones, white ones, pink ones, blue ones, and even a lime-green one (which Sebastiano declared brought out the 'col' in my cheeks).

The purpose of all this dress-trying-on business was to choose one to wear Christmas Eve during my first official televised speech to the Genovian people. I have to look regal, but not too regal. Beautiful, but not too beautiful. Sophisticated, but not too sophisticated.

I tell you, it was a nightmare of hollow-cheeked women in white (the new black) buttoning and zipping and snapping me in and out of dresses. Now I know how all those supermodels must feel. No wonder they do so many drugs.

Actually, it *was* kind of hard to choose my dress for my first big televised event because, surprisingly, Sebastiano turns out to be a pretty good designer. There were several dresses I actually wouldn't be embarrassed to be caught dead in.

Oops. Slip of the tongue. I wonder, though, if Sebastiano really does want to kill me.

He seems to like being a fashion designer, which he couldn't do if he were Prince of Genovia: he'd be too busy turning bills into law and stuff like that.

Still, you can tell he'd totally enjoy wearing a crown. Not that, as ruler of Genovia, he'd ever get to do this. I've never seen my dad in a crown. Just suits, mainly Armani.

And shorts when he plays racquetball with other world leaders.

Ew, I wonder if I will have to learn to play racquetball.

But if Sebastiano became prince of Genovia, he would totally wear a crown all the time. He told me nothing brings out the sparkles in someone's eyes like pear-shaped diamonds. He prefers Tiffany's. Or as he calls it, Tiff's.

Since we were getting so chummy and all, I told Sebastiano about the Non-Denominational Winter Dance and how I have nothing to wear to it. Sebastiano seemed disappointed when he learned I would not be wearing a tiara to my school dance, but he got over it and started asking me all these questions about the event. Like 'Who do you go with?' and 'What he look like?' and stuff like that.

I don't know what it was, but I found myself actually telling Sebastiano all about my love life. It was so weird. I totally didn't want to, but it all just started spilling out. Thank God Grandmere wasn't there . . . she'd gone off in search of more cigarettes and to have her Sidecar refreshed.

I told Sebastiano all about Kenny and how he loves me but I don't love him, and how I actually like someone else but he doesn't know I'm alive.

Sebastiano is really quite a good listener. I don't know how much, if anything, he understood about what I said, but he didn't take his eyes off my reflection as I talked, and when I was done he looked me up and down in the mirror and just said one thing: 'This boy you like. How you know he no like you back?'

'Because,' I said. 'He likes this other girl.'

Sebastiano made an impatient motion with his hands. The gesture was made more dramatic by the fact that he was wearing sleeves with these big frilly lace cuffs.

'No, no, no, no, no,' he said. 'He help you with your Al

home. He like you or he no do that. Why he do that if he no like you?'

I thought for a minute about why Michael had always been so willing to do that. Help me with my Algebra, I mean. I guess just because I am his sister's best friend and he isn't the type of person who can sit around and watch his sister's best friend flunk out of high school without, you know, at least trying to do something about it.

While I was thinking about that, I couldn't help remembering how Michael's knees, beneath our desks, sometimes brush against mine as he's telling me about integers. Or how sometimes he leans so close to correct something I've written wrong that I can smell the nice, clean scent of his soap. Or how sometimes, like when I do my Lana Weinberger imitation or whatever, he throws back his head and laughs.

Michael's lips look extra nice when he is smiling.

'Tell Sebastiano,' Sebastiano urged me. 'Tell Sebastiano why this boy helps you if he no like you.'

I sighed. 'Because I'm his little sister's best friend,' I said sadly. Really, could there *be* anything more humiliating? I mean, clearly Michael has never been impressed with my keen intellect or ravishing good looks, given my low grade point average and of course my gigantism.

Sebastiano tugged on my sleeve and went, 'You no worry. I make dress for dance. This boy, he no think of you as little sister's best friend.'

Yeah. Sure. Whatever. Why must all my relatives be so weird?

Anyway, we picked out what I'm going to wear for my introduction on Genovian national TV. It's this white taffeta job with a huge poofy skirt and this light-blue sash (the royal colours are blue and white). But Sebastiano had one of his assistants take photos of me in all the dresses so I can see

106

how I look in them and then decide. I thought this was fairly professional for a guy who calls breakfast 'breck'.

But all that isn't what I want to write about although I'm so tired I hardly know what I'm doing. What I want to write about is what happened today after Algebra review.

Which was that Mr Gianini, after everyone but me had left, went, 'Mia, I heard a rumour that there was supposed to be some kind of student walkout today. Had you heard that?'

Me:	(*Freezing in my seat*) Um, no.
Mr Gianini:	Oh. So you wouldn't know then if somebody – maybe in protest at the protest – threw the second-floor fire alarm? The one by the drinking fountain?
Me:	(*Wishing Lars would stop coughing suggestively*) Um, no.
Mr Gianini:	That's what I thought. Because you know the penalty for pulling one of the fire alarms – when there is, in fact, no sign of a fire – is expulsion.
Me:	Oh, yes. I know that.
Mr Gianini:	I thought you might have seen who did it, since I believe I gave you a hall pass shortly before the alarm went off.
Me:	Oh, no. I didn't see anybody.

Except Justin Baxendale, and his smoky eyelashes. But I didn't say that.

Mr Gianini:	I didn't think so. Oh, well. If you ever hear who did it, maybe you could tell her from me never to do it again.
Me:	Um. OK.
Mr Gianini:	And tell her thanks from me too. The last thing we need right now, with tensions running so

high over Finals, is a student walkout. (*Mr Gianini picked up his briefcase and jacket.*) See you at home.

Then he winked at me. WINKED at me, like he knew I was the one who'd done it. But he couldn't know. I mean, he doesn't know about my nostrils (which were fully flaring the whole time; I could *feel* them!) Right? RIGHT????

Thursday, December 10, Homeroom

Lilly is going to drive me crazy.

Seriously. Like it's not enough I have Finals and my introduction to Genovia and my love life and everything to worry about. I have to listen to Lilly complain about how the administration of Albert Einstein High is out to get her. The whole way to school this morning she just droned on and on about how it's all a plot to silence her because she once complained about the Coke machine outside the gym. Apparently, the Coke machine is indicative of the administration's efforts to turn us all into mindless soda-drinking, Gap-wearing clones.

If you ask me, this isn't really about Coke, or the attempts by the school's administration to turn us into mindless pod-people. It's really just because Lilly's still mad she can't use a chapter of the book she's writing on the teen experience as her term paper.

I told Lilly if she doesn't submit a new topic, she's going to get an F as her nine-week grade. Factored in with her A for the last nine weeks, that's only like a C, which will significantly lower her grade point average and put her chances of getting into Berkeley, which is her first-choice school, at risk. She may be forced to fall back on her safety school, Brown, which I know would be quite a blow.

She didn't even listen to me. She says she's having an organizational meeting of this new group (of which she is president) Students Against the Corporatization of Albert Einstein High School (SACAEHS) on Saturday, and I have to come because I am the group's secretary. Don't ask me how *that* happened. Lilly says I write everything down anyway so it shouldn't be any trouble for me.

I wish Michael had been there to defend me from his

sister but, like he has every day this week, he took the subway to school early so he can work on his project for the Winter Carnival.

I wouldn't doubt Judith Gershner has been showing up at school on the early side too, this week.

Speaking of Michael, I picked up another greeting card, this one from the Plaza gift shop, on the way to Sebastiano's showroom last night. It's a lot better than that stupid one with the strawberry. This one has a picture of a lady holding a finger to her lips. Inside it says, *Shhhh . . .*

Under that, I am having Tina write:

Roses are red
But cherries are redder
Maybe she can clone fruit flies
But I like you better.

What I meant was that I like him more than Judith Gershner does, but I'm not really sure that comes through in the poem. Tina says it does, but Tina thinks I should have used love instead of like, so who knows if her opinion is of any value? This is a poem clearly calling for a like and not a love.

I should know. I write enough of them.

Poems, I mean.

110

English Journal

This semester we have read several novels, including To Kill a Mockingbird, Huckleberry Finn *and* The Scarlet Letter. *In your English journal please record your feelings about the books we have read, and books in general. What have been your most meaningful experiences as a reader? Your favourite books? Your least favourite?*

Please utilize transitive sentences.

Books I Have Read, and
What They Meant to Me
by Mia Thermopolis

Books That Were Good

1. Jaws – *I bet you didn't know that in the book version of this, Richard Dreyfuss and Roy Scheider's wife have sex. But they do.*
2. The Catcher in the Rye – *This is totally good. It has lots of bad words.*
3. To Kill a Mockingbird – *This is an excellent book. They should do a movie version of this with Mel Gibson as Atticus, and he should blow Mr Ewell away with a flame thrower at the end.*
4. A Wrinkle in Time – *Only we never find out the most important thing: whether or not Meg has breasts. I'm thinking she probably did, considering the fact that she already had the glasses and braces. I mean, all of that and flat-chested too? God wouldn't be so cruel.*
5. Emanuelle – *In the eighth grade, my best friend and I found this book on top of a rubbish bin on East Third Street. We took turns reading it out loud. It was very, very good. At least the parts I remember. My mom caught us reading it and took it away before we'd gotten a chance to finish it.*

Books That Sucked*

1. The Scarlet Letter – *You know what would have been cool? If there had been a rift in the space–time continuum and one of those Euro-trash terrorists Bruce Willis is always chasing in the* Die Hard *movies dropped a nuclear bomb on the town where Arthur Dimmesdale and all those losers lived, and blew it sky high. That's about the only thing I can think of that would have made this book even remotely interesting.*

2. Our Town – *OK, this is a play and not a book, but they still made us read it and all I have to say about it is that, basically, you find out when you die that nobody cared about you and we're all alone for ever, the end. OK! Thanks for that! I feel much better now!*

3. The Mill on the Floss – *I don't want to give anything away here, but midway through the book, just when things were going good and there were all these hot romances (not as hot as in* Emanuelle, *though, so don't get your hopes up), someone very crucial to the plot DIES, which if you ask me is just a cop-out so the author could make her deadline on time.*

4. Anne of Green Gables – *All that blah-blah-blah about imagination. I tried to imagine some car chases or explosions that would actually make this book good, but I must be like all of Anne's drippy unimaginative friends, because I couldn't.*

5. Little House on the Prairie – *Little yawn on the big snore. I have all ninety-seven thousand of these books because people kept on giving them to me when I was little and all I have to say is if Half Pint had lived in Manhattan, she'd have gotten her you-know-what kicked from here to Avenue D.*

* Mrs Spears, I believe the word 'sucked' is transitive in this instance.

112

Thursday, December 10, Fourth Period

No PE today!

Instead there is an Assembly.

And it's not because there's a sporting event they want us all to show our support for. No! This is no pep rally. There isn't a cheerleader in sight. Well, OK, there are cheerleaders in sight, but they aren't in uniform or anything. They are sitting in the bleachers with the rest of us. Well, not really with the rest of us since they are in the best seats, the ones in the middle, all jostling to see who can sit next to Justin Baxendale, who has apparently ousted Josh Richter as hottest guy in school, but whatever.

No. Instead, it appears that there has been a major disciplinary infraction at Albert Einstein High School. An act of random vandalism that has shaken the administration's faith in us. Which is why they called an Assembly, so that they could better convey their feelings of – as Lilly just whispered in my ear – disillusionment and betrayal.

And what was this act that has Principal Gupta and the trustees so up in arms?

Why, someone pulled a fire alarm yesterday, that's what.

Oops.

I have to say, I have never done anything really bad before – well, I dropped an eggplant out of a fifteenth-floor window a couple of months ago, but no one got hurt or anything – but there really is something sort of thrilling about it. I mean, I would never want to do anything *too* bad – like anything where someone might get hurt.

But I have to say, it is immensely gratifying to have all these people coming up to the microphone and decrying my behaviour.

I probably wouldn't feel so good about it if I'd gotten caught, though.

I am being urged to come forward and turn myself in even as I write this. Apparently, the guilt for my action is going to hound me well past my teen years – possibly even into my twenties and beyond.

OK, can I just tell you how much I'm NOT going to think about high school when I am in my twenties? I am going to be way too busy working with Greenpeace to save the whales to worry about some stupid fire alarm I pulled in the ninth grade.

The administration is offering a reward for information leading to the identity of the perpetrator of this heinous crime. A reward! You know what the reward is? A free movie pass to the Sony Imax theatre. That's all I'm worth! A movie pass!

The only person who could possibly turn me in isn't even paying attention to the Assembly. I can see Justin Baxendale has got a Gameboy out and is playing it with the sound off while Lana and her fellow cheer cronies look over his broad shoulders, probably panting so hard they are fogging up the screen.

I guess Justin hasn't put two and two together yet. You know, about seeing me in the hallway just before that fire alarm went off. With any luck, he never will.

Mr Gianini, though. That's another story. I see him over there, talking to Mrs Hill. He has obviously not told anyone that he suspects me.

Maybe he doesn't suspect me. Maybe he thinks Lilly did it and I know about it. That could be. I can tell Lilly really wishes she'd done it because she keeps on muttering under her breath about how when she finds out who did it, she's going to kill that person, etc.

She's just jealous, of course. That's because now it seems like some kind of political statement, instead of what it actually was: a way to prevent a political statement.

Principal Gupta is looking at us very sternly. She says that it is always natural to want to burn off a little steam right before Finals, but that she hopes we will choose positive channels for this, such as the penny drive the Community Outreach Club is holding in order to benefit the victims of Tropical Storm Fred, which flooded several suburban New Jersey neighbourhoods last November.

Ha! As if contributing to a stupid penny drive can ever give anybody the same kind of thrill as committing a completely random act of civil disobedience.

Thursday, December 10, Gifted and Talented

Today was my lunch with Kenny at Big Wong.

I really don't have anything to say about it, except that he didn't ask me to the Non-Denominational Winter Dance. Not only that, but it appears that Kenny's passion for me has ebbed significantly since it hit its zenith on Tuesday.

I, of course, was beginning to suspect this, since he's stopped calling me after school and I haven't had one Instant Message from him since before the great Ice-skating Debacle. He says it's because he's so busy studying for Finals and all, but I suspect something else:

He knows. He knows about Michael.

I mean, come on. How can he not?

Well, OK, maybe he doesn't know about Michael *specifically*, but Kenny must know *generally* that he is not the one who lights my fire.

If I had a fire, that is.

No, Kenny is just being nice.

Which I appreciate and all, but I just wish he'd come out and say it. All this kindness, this solicitousness – it's just making me feel worse. I mean, really? How could I have ever agreed to be Kenny's girlfriend, knowing full well I liked someone else? By rights, Kenny should go to *Majesty* magazine and spill all. *Royal Betrayal*, they could call it. I totally would understand it, if he did.

But he won't. Because he's too nice.

Instead, he ordered steamed vegetable dumplings for me and pork buns for him (one encouraging sign that Kenny might not love me as much as he used to insist: he's eating meat again) and talked about Bio. and what had happened at Assembly (I didn't tell him it was me who pulled the alarm and he didn't ask me, so there was no need shield my nostrils). He mentioned again how sorry he was about my tongue, and asked how I was doing in Algebra, and offered to come over and tutor me if I wanted (Kenny tested out of freshman Algebra), even though of course I live with an Algebra teacher. Still, you could tell he meant to be nice.

Which just makes me feel worse. Because of what I'm going to have to do after Finals and all.

But he didn't ask me to the dance.

I don't know if this means we aren't going, or if it means he considers the fact we are going a given.

I swear, I do not understand boys at all.

As if lunch wasn't bad enough, G & T isn't too great, either. No, Judith Gershner isn't here . . . but neither is Michael. The guy is AWOL. Nobody knows where he is. Lilly had to tell Mrs Hill, when she took attendance, that her brother was in the bathroom.

I wonder where he really is. Lilly says that since he started writing this new program that the Computer Club will be unveiling at the Winter Carnival, she's hardly seen him.

Which is no real change since Michael hardly comes out of his room anyway, but still. You'd think he'd come home once in a while to study.

But I guess, seeing as how he already got into his first-choice college, his grades don't really matter any more.

Besides, like Lilly, Michael is a genius. What does he need to study for?

Unlike the rest of us slobs.

I wish they'd put the door back on the supply closet. It is extremely hard to concentrate with Boris scraping away on his violin in there. Lilly says this is just another tactic by the trustees to weaken our resistance so we will remain the mindless drones they are trying to make us, but I think it's on account of that time we all forgot to let him out and he

117

was stuck in there until the night custodian heard his anguished pleas to be released.

Which is Lilly's fault, if you think about it. I mean, she's his girlfriend. She should really take better care of him.

Homework:

Algebra: practice test
English: term paper
World Civ.: practice test
G & T: none
French: l'examen pratique
Biology: practice test

Thursday, December 10, 9 p.m.

Grandmere is seriously out of control. Tonight she started quizzing me on the names and responsibilities of all of my dad's cabinet ministers. Not only do I have to know exactly what they do, but also their marital status and the names and ages of their kids, if any. These are the kids I am supposedly going to have to hang out with while celebrating Christmas at the Palace. I am figuring they will probably hate me as much, if not more, than Mr Gianini's niece and nephew hated me at Thanksgiving.

All of my holidays from now on are apparently going to be spent in the company of teens who hate me.

You know, I would just like to say that it is totally not my fault I am a princess. They have no right to hate me so much. I have done everything I could to maintain a normal life in spite of my royal status. I have totally turned down opportunities to be on the covers of *CosmoGirl, Teen People, Seventeen, YM* and *Girl's Life*. I have refused invitations to go on *TRL* and introduce the number one video in the country, and when the mayor asked if I wanted to be the one to press the button that drops the ball in Times Square on New Year's Eve, I said no (aside from the fact I am going to be in Genovia for New Year's, I oppose the Mayor's mosquito-spraying campaign, as runoff from the pesticides used to kill the mosquitoes that may be carrying the West Nile virus has infected the local horseshoe crab population. A compound in the blood of horseshoe crabs, which nest all along the eastern seaboard, is used to test the purity of every drug and vaccine administered in the U.S. The crabs are routinely gathered, drained of a third of their blood, then re-released into the sea . . . a sea which is now killing them, as well as many other

119

arthropods, such as lobsters, thanks to the amount of pesticide in it).

Anyway, I am just saying, all the kids who hate me should chill because I have never once sought the spotlight I have been thrust into. I've never even called my own press conference.

But I digress.

So Sebastiano was there, with Grandmere, drinking aperitifs and listening as I rattled off name after name (Grandmere has made flashcards out of the pictures of the cabinet ministers – kind of like those bubble gum cards you can get of the Backstreet Boys, only the cabinet ministers don't wear as much leather). I was kind of thinking maybe I was wrong about Sebastiano's commitment to fashion, and that maybe he was there to try and pick up some pointers for after he's thrust me into the path of an oncoming limo or whatever.

But when Grandmere paused to take a phone call from her old friend General Pinochet, Sebastiano started asking me all these questions about clothes, in particular what clothes my friends and I like to wear. What were my feelings, he wanted to know, on velvet stretch trousers? Spandex tube-tops? Sequins?

I told him all of that sounded, you know, OK for Halloween or Jersey City, but that generally in my day-to-day life I prefer cotton. He looked saddened by this, so I told him that I really felt orange was going to be the next pink and that perked him right up, and he wrote a bunch of stuff down in this notebook he carries around. Kind of like I do, now that I think about it.

When Grandmere got off the phone, I informed her – quite diplomatically, I might add – that, considering how much progress we'd made in the past two months, I felt more than prepared for my impending introduction to the people of Genovia, and that I did not feel it would be necessary to have lessons next week as I have SIX finals to prepare for.

But Grandmere got totally huffy about it! She was all, 'Where did you get the idea that your academic education is more important than your royal training? Your father, I suppose. With him, it's always education, education, education. He doesn't realize that education is nowhere near as important as deportment.'

'Grandmere,' I said. 'I need an education if I'm going to run Genovia properly.' Especially if I'm going to convert the palace into a giant animal shelter – something I'm not going to be able to do until Grandmere is dead, so I see no point in mentioning it to her now . . . or ever, for that matter.

Grandmere said some swear words in French, which wasn't very dowager-princessy of her, if you ask me. Thankfully, right then my dad walked in, looking for his Genovian Air Force medal since he had a state dinner to go to over at the Embassy. I told him about my Finals and how I really needed time off from princess stuff to study, and he was all, 'Yes, of course.'

When Grandmere protested, he just went, 'For God's sake, if she hasn't got it by now, she never will.'

Grandmere pressed her lips together and didn't say anything more after that. Sebastiano used the opportunity to ask me about my feelings on rayon. I told him I didn't have any.

For once, I was telling the truth.

Friday, December 11, Homeroom

Here's what I have to do:

1. Stop thinking about Michael, especially when I should be studying.
2. Stop telling Grandmere anything about my personal life.
3. Start acting more:
   A. Mature
   B. Responsible
   C. Regal
4. Stop biting my fingernails.
5. Write down everything Mom and Mr G need to know about how to take care of Fat Louie while I'm gone.
6. CHRISTMAS/HANUKKAH PRESENTS!
7. Stop watching *Baywatch* when I should be studying.
8. Stop playing Pod-Racer when I should be studying.
9. Stop listening to music when I should be studying.
10. Break up with Kenny.

Friday, December 11, Principal Gupta's Office

Well, I guess it's official now:

I, Mia Thermopolis, am a juvenile delinquent.

Seriously. That fire alarm I pulled was only the beginning, it appears.

I really don't know what's come over me lately. It's like the closer I get to actually going to Genovia and performing my first official duties as its princess, the less like a princess I act.

I wonder if I'll be expelled.

If I am, it is totally unfair. Lana started it. I was sitting there in Algebra, listening to Mr G go on about the Cartesian plane, when suddenly Lana turns around in her seat and slaps a copy of *USA Today* down in front of me. There is a headline screaming:

Today's Poll

Most Popular Young Royal

Fifty-seven per cent of readers say that **Prince William of England** is their favourite young royal, with Will's little brother **Harry** coming in at twenty-eight per cent. America's own royal, **Princess Mia Renaldo of Genovia**, comes in third, with thirteen per cent of the votes, and Prince Andrew and Sarah Ferguson's daughters, **Beatrice** and **Eugenie**, round out the votes with one per cent each.

The reasons given for Princess Mia's lack of popularity? 'Not out-going' is the most common answer. Ironically, Princess Mia is perceived as being as shy as Princess Diana – the mother of William and Harry – when she first stepped into the harsh glare of the media spotlight.

Princess Mia, who only recently learned she was heir to the throne of Genovia, a small principality located just off the Cote d'Azur, is expected to make her first official trip to that country in her capacity as its future ruler next week. A representative for the princess describes her as looking forward to her visit with 'eager anticipation'. The princess will continue her education in America and reside in Genovia only during the summer months.

I read the stupid article and then passed the paper back to Lana.

'So?' I whispered to her.

'So,' Lana whispered. 'I wonder how popular you'd be – especially with the people of Genovia – if they found out their future ruler goes around pulling fire alarms when there isn't any fire.'

She was only guessing, of course. She couldn't have seen me. Unless . . .

Unless Justin Baxendale *did* figure it out – you know, seeing me in the hallway like that just before the alarm went off – and mentioned it to Lana . . .

No. Not possible. I am so far out of the sphere of Justin Baxendale's consciousness as to be non-existent to him. Lana, like Mr G, obviously just thinks it's a little coincidental that on that fateful Wednesday the fire alarm went off about two minutes after I'd disappeared from class with the pass to the bathroom.

But even so. Even though she could only have been guessing, it seemed to me like she knew and was going to make sure I never heard the end of it.

I really don't know what came over me. I don't know if it was:

A. The stress of Finals.
B. My impending trip to Genovia.
C. This thing with Kenny.
D. The fact that I'm in love with this guy who is going out with a human fruit fly.
E. The fact that my mother is going to give birth to my Algebra teacher's baby.
F. The fact that Lana has been persecuting me practically my whole life and pretty much getting away with it, or
All of the above.

Whatever the reason was, I snapped. Just snapped. Suddenly, I found myself reaching for Lana's mobile, which was lying on her desktop beside her calculator.

And then the next thing I knew, I had put the tiny little pink thing on the floor and crushed it into a lot of pieces beneath the heel of my size eight combat boot.

I guess I can't really blame Mr G for sending me to the principal's office.

Still, you would expect a little sympathy from your own stepfather.

Uh oh. Here comes Principal Gupta.

Friday, December 11, 5 p.m., the Loft

Well, that's it, then. I'm suspended.

Suspended. I can't believe it. ME! Mia Thermopolis! What is happening to me? I used to be such a good kid!

And, OK, it's just for one day, but still. It's going on my permanent record! What are the Genovian cabinet ministers going to say?

I am turning into Courtney Love.

And, yeah, it's not like I'm not going to get into college because I was suspended for one day in the first semester of my freshman year, but how totally embarrassing! Principal Gupta treated me like I was some kind of *criminal* or something.

And you know what they say: treat a person like a criminal and pretty soon she'll end up behaving like one. At least, I think that's what they say. The way things are going, I wouldn't be surprised if pretty soon I start wearing ripped-up fishnet stockings and dyeing my hair black. Maybe I'll even start smoking and get my ears double-pierced or something. And then they'll make a TV movie about me and call it *Royal Scandal*. It will show me going up to Prince William and saying, 'Who's the most popular young royal now, huh, punk?' and then headbutting him or something.

Except I practically fainted the first time I got my ears pierced, and smoking is really bad for you, and I always thought it must hurt to headbutt someone.

I guess I don't have the makings of a juvenile delinquent after all.

My dad doesn't think so, either. He's all ready to set the royal Genovian lawyers on Principal Gupta. The only problem, of course, is that I won't tell him – or anybody else, for that matter – what Lana said to make me assault her mobile.

It's kind of hard to prove the attack was provoked if the attacker won't say what the provocation was. My dad pleaded with me for a while when he came to pick me up from school, after having received The Call from Principal Gupta. But when I wouldn't tell him what he wanted, and Lars just looked carefully blank, my dad just went, 'Fine', and his mouth got all scrunchy like it does when Grandmere has one too many Sidecars and starts calling him Papa Cueball.

But how can I tell him what Lana said? If I do that, then everyone will know I'm guilty of not just one crime, but two!

Anyway, now I'm home, watching the Lifetime channel with my mother. She hasn't been doing much painting at her studio since she got pregnant. This is on account of her being exhausted. It's quite hard to paint lying down, she's discovered. So instead she has been doing a lot of sketching in bed – mostly line drawings of Fat Louie, who seems to enjoy having someone home all day with him. He sits for hours on her bed, watching the pigeons on the fire escape outside her window.

But since I'm home today, Mom did some drawings of me. I think she is making my mouth too big, but I'm not saying anything as Mr Gianini and I have discovered it's better not to upset my mother in her current hormonal state. Even the slightest criticism – like asking her why she left the phone bill in the vegetable crisper – can lead to hour-long crying jags.

While she sketched me, I watched a very excellent movie called *Mother, May I Sleep with Danger?* starring Tori Spelling of *Beverly Hills 90210* fame, as a girl who has an abusive boyfriend. I really don't get why any girl would stay with a guy who hits her, but my mom says it's all about self-esteem and your relationship with your father. Except that my mom doesn't have that great a relationship with Papaw, my grandfather, and if any guy ever tried to slug her, you can bet she'd put him in the hospital, so go figure.

As my mom drew, she tried to get me to spill my guts to her – you know, about what Lana said that made me go on a mobile-stomping rampage. You could tell she was trying really hard to be all TV mom about it.

And I guess it must have worked because all of a sudden I found myself telling her all of it, every last thing: the stuff about Kenny and about my not liking to kiss him, and about him telling everybody that, and about how I plan to break up with him as soon as Finals are over.

And along the way I mentioned Michael, and Judith Gershner, and Tina and the greeting cards, and the Winter Carnival, and Lilly and her protest and how I'm secretary of it, and just about everything else, except the part about pulling the fire alarm.

And after a while my mom stopped drawing and just looked at me.

Finally, when I was done, she said, 'You know what I think you need?'

And I said, 'What?'

And she said, 'A vacation.'

So then we had a sort of vacation, right there on her bed. I mean, she wouldn't let me go and study. Instead, she made me order a pizza and together we watched the satisfying but completely unbelievable end of *Mother, May I Sleep with Danger?*, which was followed, much to our joy, by the dishiest made-for-TV movie ever, *Midwest Obsession*, in which Courtney Thorne Smith plays the local Dairy Princess who goes around in a pink Cadillac wearing cow earrings, killing people like Tracey Gold (deep in the throes of her post *Growing Pains* anorexia) for messing with her boyfriend.

And the best part was, it was all *based on a true story.*

For a while, there on my mom's bed, it was almost like old times. You know, before my mom met Mr Gianini and I found out I was a princess.

Except, of course, not really, because she's pregnant and I'm suspended.

But why quibble?

Friday, December 11, 8 p.m., the Loft

Oh my God, I just checked my e-mail. I am being inundated with supportive messages from my friends!

They all want to congratulate me on my decisive handling of Lana Weinberger. They sympathize with my suspension and encourage me to stay firm in my refusal to back down from my stand against the administration (what stand against the administration? All I did was destroy a mobile phone. It has nothing to do with the administration). Lilly went so far as to compare me to Mary Queen of Scots, who was imprisoned and then beheaded by Elizabeth the First.

I wonder if Lilly would still think that if she knew that the reason I smashed Lana's mobile was because she was threatening to spill the beans about my having pulled the fire alarm that ruined Lilly's walkout.

Lilly says it's all a matter of principle – that I was banished from the school for refusing to back down from my beliefs. But actually, I was banished from school for destroying someone else's private property – and I only did it to cover up for another crime that I committed.

No one knows that but me, though. Well, me and Lana. And even she doesn't know for sure why I did it. I mean, it could have been just one of those random acts of violence that are going around.

Everyone else, however, is seeing it as this great political act. Tomorrow, at the first meeting of the Students Against the Corporatization of Albert Einstein High School, my case is going to be held up as an example of one of the many unjust decisions of the Gupta administration.

I think tomorrow I might develop a case of weekend strep throat.

Anyway, I wrote back to everyone, telling them how much

I appreciate their support but not to make a bigger deal out of this than it actually is. I mean, I'm not proud of what I did. I would much rather have NOT done it and stayed in school.

One bright note: Michael is definitely getting the cards I've been sending him. Tina walked by his locker today after PE and saw him take the latest one out and put it in his backpack! Unfortunately, according to Tina, he did not wear an expression of dazed passion as he slipped the card into his bag, nor did he gaze at it tenderly. He did not even put it away very carefully. Tina regretted to inform me that he slipped his Imac laptop into his backpack next, undoubtedly squashing the card.

But he wouldn't, Tina hastened to assure me, have done that if he'd known it was from you, Mia! Maybe if you'd signed it . . .

But if I signed it, he'd know I like him! More than that, he'd know I love him, since I do believe the L word was mentioned in at least one card. And what if he doesn't feel the same way about me? How embarrassing! Way worse than being suspended.

Oh, no! As I was writing this, I got Instant Messaged by, of all people, Michael himself! I freaked out so bad that I shrieked and scared Fat Louie, who was sleeping on my lap as I wrote. He sank all of his claws into me, and now I have little puncture marks all over my thighs.

Michael wrote:

```
CracKing: Hey, Thermopolis, what's this I hear
about you getting suspended?
```

I wrote back:

```
FtLouie: Just for one day.
>
```

CracKing: What'd you do?
>
FtLouie: Crushed a cheerleader's mobile phone.
>
CracKing: Your parents must be so proud.
>
FtLouie: If so, they've done a pretty good job
of disguising it so far.
>
CracKing: So, are you grounded?
>
FtLouie: Surprisingly, no. I told them the
attack on the phone was provoked.
>
CracKing: So you'll still be going to the
Carnival next week?
>
FtLouie: As secretary to the Students Against
the Corporatization of Albert Einstein High
School, I believe my attendance is required.
Your sister is planning for us to have a booth.
>
CracKing: That Lilly. She's always looking out
for the good of mankind.
>
FtLouie: That's one way of putting it.

We probably would have talked longer, but right then my
mom yelled at me to get offline, since she's waiting to hear
from Mr Gianini, who, surprisingly, still isn't home from
school, even though it is past dinnertime. So I logged off.

This is the second time Michael's asked if I'm going to the
Winter Carnival. What is up with that?

Friday, December 11, 9 p.m., the Loft

Now we know why Mr G was so late getting home:

He stopped along the way to buy a Christmas tree.

Not just any Christmas tree, either, but a twelve-footer that must be at least six feet wide at the base.

I didn't say anything negative, of course, because my mom was so happy and excited about it and immediately lugged out all of her Dead Celebrity Christmas ornaments (my mom doesn't use pretty glass balls or tinsel on her Christmas tree, like normal people. Instead, she paints pieces of tin with the likenesses of celebrities that have died that year and hangs those on the tree. (Which is why we probably have the only tree in North America with ornaments commemorating Richard and Pat Nixon, Elvis, Audrey Hepburn, Kurt Cobain, Jim Henson, John Belushi, Rock Hudson, Alec Guiness, Divine, John Lennon and many, many more.)

Mr Gianini kept looking over at me, to see if I was happy too. He got the tree, he said, because he knew what a bad day I'd had and he didn't want it to be a total loss.

Mr G, of course, has no idea what my English term paper topic is.

What was I supposed to say? I mean, he'd already gone out and bought it, and you know a tree that size had to have cost a lot of money. And he'd meant to do a nice thing. He really had.

Still, I wish the people around here would consult me about things before just going out and doing them. Like the whole pregnancy thing, and now this tree. If Mr G had asked me, I would have been like, Let's go to the Big K Mart on Astor Place and get a nice fake tree so we don't contribute to the destruction of the polar bear's natural habitat, OK?

133

Only he didn't ask me.

And the truth is, even if he did, my mom would never have gone for it. Her favourite part of Christmas is lying on the floor with her head under the tree, gazing up through the branches and inhaling the sweet tangy smell of pine sap. She says it's the only memory of her Indiana childhood she actually likes.

It's hard to think about the polar bears when your mom says something like that.

Saturday, December 12, 2 p.m., Lilly's Apartment

Well, the first meeting of the Students Against the Corporatization of Albert Einstein High School is a complete bust.

That's because nobody showed up but me and Boris Pelkowski. I am a little miffed that Kenny didn't come. You would think that if he really loves me as much as he says he does, he would take any opportunity whatsoever to be near me, even a boring meeting of the Students Against the Corporatization of Albert Einstein High School.

But I guess even Kenny's love is not that great. As should be obvious to me by now, considering the fact that there are exactly six days until the Non-Denominational Winter Dance, and Kenny STILL HASN'T ASKED ME IF I WANT TO GO WITH HIM.

Not that I'm worried, or anything. I mean, does a girl who set off a fire alarm AND smashed Lana Weinberger's mobile worry about not having a date to a stupid dance?

All right. I'm worried.

But not worried enough to completely humiliate myself and ask *him* to the dance.

Lilly is pretty much inconsolable over the fact that no one but Boris and me showed up to her meeting. I tried to tell her that everybody is too busy studying for Finals to worry about privatization at the moment, but she doesn't seem to care. Right now she is sitting on the couch with Boris speaking to her in a soothing voice. Boris is pretty gross and all – with his sweaters that he always tucks into his trousers, and that weird brace his orthodontist makes him wear – but you can tell he genuinely loves Lilly. I mean, look at the tender way he is gazing at her as she sobs about how she is going to call her congressperson.

It makes my heart hurt, looking at Boris look at Lilly.

I guess I must be jealous. I want a boy to look at *me* like that. And I don't mean Kenny, either. I mean a boy who I actually like back, as more than just a friend.

I can't take it any more. I am going into the kitchen to see what Maya, the Moscovitzes' housekeeper, is doing. Even helping to wash things has to be better than this.

Saturday, December 12, 2:30 p.m.,
Lilly's Apartment

Maya wasn't in the kitchen. She was here, in Michael's room, putting away his school uniform which she just finished ironing. Maya is going around picking up Michael's things and telling me about her son Manuel. Thanks to the help of the Drs Moscovitz, Manuel was recently released from the prison in the Dominican Republic where he'd been wrongfully held on suspicion of having committed crimes against the state. Now Manuel is starting his own political party and Maya is just as proud as can be, except she is worried he might end up back in prison if he doesn't tone down the anti-government stuff a little.

Manuel and Lilly have a lot in common, I guess.

Maya's stories about Manuel are always interesting, but it is much more interesting to be in Michael's room. I have been in it before, of course, but never while he was gone (he is at school even though it is Saturday, working in the computer lab on his project for the carnival; apparently, the school's modem is faster than his. Also, I suppose, though I hate to admit it, he and Judith Gershner can freely practice their downloading there, without fear of parental interruption).

So I am lying on Michael's bed while Maya putters around, folding shirts and muttering about sugar, one of her native land's main exports and, apparently, a source of some consternation to her son's political platform, while Michael's dog, Pavlov, sits next to me, panting on my face. I can't help thinking, *This is what it would be like to be Michael. This is what Michael sees when he looks up at his ceiling at night* (he has put glow-in-the-dark stars up there, in the form of the spiral

137

galaxy Andromeda) and *This is how Michael's sheets smell* (springtime fresh, thanks to the detergent Maya uses) and *This is what the view of Michael's desk looks like from his bed.*

Except that looking over at his desk, I just noticed something. It's one of my cards! The one with the strawberry on it!

It isn't exactly on display, or anything. It's just sitting on his desk. But hey, that's a far cry from being crumpled at the bottom of his backpack. It shows that the cards mean something to him, that he hasn't just buried them under all the other junk on his desk – the DOS manuals and anti-Microsoft literature . . . or worse, thrown them away.

This is somewhat heartening.

Uh-oh. I just heard the front door open. Michael??? Or the Drs Moscovitz???? I better get out of here. Michael doesn't have all those 'Enter At Your Own Risk' signs on the door for nothing.

Saturday, December 12, 3 p.m., Grandmere's

How, you might ask, did I go from the Moscovitzes' apartment to my grandmother's suite at the Plaza in the space of a mere half hour?

Well, I'll tell you.

Disaster has struck, in the form of Sebastiano.

I always suspected, of course, that Sebastiano was not the sweet-tempered innocent he pretended to be. But now it looks like the only murder Sebastiano needs to worry about is his own. Because if my dad ever gets his hands on him, Sebastiano is one dead fashion designer.

Looking at it objectively, I think I can safely say I'd prefer to have been murdered. I mean, I'd be dead and all, which would be sad – especially since I still haven't written down those instructions for caring for Fat Louie while I'm gone – but at least I wouldn't have to show up for school on Monday.

But now, not only do I have to show up for school on Monday, but I have to show up for school on Monday knowing that every single one of my fellow classmates is going to have seen the supplement that arrived in the *Sunday Times*: the supplement featuring about twenty photos of ME standing in front of a triple mirror in dresses by Sebastiano, with the words *Fashion Fit for a Princess* emblazoned all over the place.

Oh, yes. I'm not kidding. *Fashion Fit for a Princess.*

I can't really blame him, I guess. Sebastiano, I mean. I suppose the opportunity was too much for him to resist. He is, after all, a businessman, and having a princess model your clothes . . . well, you can't buy exposure like that.

Because you know all the other papers are going to pick up on the story. You know, Princess of Genovia Makes Modelling Debut. That kind of thing.

So with just one little photo spread, Sebastiano is going to get virtually worldwide coverage of his new clothing line.

A clothing line that it looks like I have endorsed.

Grandmere doesn't understand why my dad and I are so upset. Well, I think she gets why my dad is upset. You know, the whole 'my daughter is being used' thing. She just doesn't get why *I'm* so unhappy. 'You look perfectly beautiful,' she keeps saying.

Yeah. Like that helps.

Grandmere thinks I am overreacting. But hello, have I ever aspired to tread in Claudia Schiffer's footsteps? I don't think so. Fashion is so not what I'm about. What about the environment? What about the rights of animals? What about the **HORSESHOE CRABS??????**

People are not going to believe I didn't pose for those photos. People are going to think I am a sellout. People are going to think I am a stuck-up model snob.

I would so rather that they think I am a juvenile delinquent, I can't tell you.

Little did I know when I heard the front door to the Moscovitzes' apartment opening, and I hustled out of Michael's room, that I was about to be greeted by the disastrous news. It was only Lilly's parents, after all, coming home from the gym where they'd met with their personal trainers. Afterwards, they'd stopped to have latte and read the Sunday paper, large sections of which arrive, for reasons no one understands, on Saturday, if you have a subscription.

What a surprise they had when they opened up the paper and saw the Princess of Genovia hawking this hot new fashion designer's spring collection.

What a surprise *I* had when the Drs Moscovitz congratulated me on my new modelling career, and I was all, 'What are you talking about?'

140

So, while Lilly and Boris looked on curiously, Dr Moscovitz opened her paper and showed me:

And there it was, in all of its four-colour-layout glory.

I'm not going to lie and say I looked bad. I looked OK. What they had done was, they had taken all the photos Sebastiano's assistant had snapped of me trying to decide which dress to wear to my introduction to the people of Genovia, and laid them all out on this purple background. I'm not smiling in the pictures or anything. I'm just looking at myself in the mirror, clearly going, in my head, *Ew, could I look more like a walking toothpick?*

But of course, if you didn't know me and didn't know WHY I was trying on all these dresses, I'd seem like some freak who cares WAY too much about how she looks in a party dress.

Which is exactly the kind of person I've always wanted to be portrayed as.

NOT!!!!!!!

I can't figure out what Sebastiano was thinking. I mean, I have to admit, I am a little hurt. I'd thought, when he'd asked me all those questions about Michael, that he and I had kind of made a connection. But I guess not. Not if he could do something like this.

My dad has already called the *Times* and demanded that they remove the supplement from all the papers that haven't been delivered yet. He has called the concierge of the Plaza and insisted on Sebastiano being listed as persona non grata, which means the cousin to the Prince of Genovia won't be allowed to set foot on hotel property.

I thought this was a little harsh, but not as harsh as what my dad wanted to do, which was call the NYPD and press charges against Sebastiano for using the likeness of a minor without the authority of her parents. Thank God

Grandmere talked him out of that. She said there'd be enough publicity about this without the added humiliation of a royal arrest.

My dad is still so mad he can't sit still. He is pacing back and forth across the suite. Rommel is watching him very nervously from Grandmere's lap, his head moving back and forth, back and forth, as his eyes follow my dad, as if he were watching the US Open.

I bet if Sebastiano *were* here, my dad would smash up a lot more than just his mobile phone.

Well.

All I can say is, Grandmere's really done it this time.

I'm serious. I don't think my dad is ever going to speak to her again.

And I know *I* never will.

OK, she's an old lady and she didn't know what she was doing was wrong, and I should really be more understanding.

But for her to do *this* – for her not even to take into consideration my feelings – I frankly don't think I will ever be able to forgive her.

What happened was, Sebastiano called right before I was getting ready to leave the hotel. He was completely perplexed about why my dad is so mad at him. He tried to come upstairs to see us, he said, but Plaza security stopped him.

When my dad, who'd answered the phone, told Sebastiano that the reason Plaza security stopped him was because he'd been PNG'd, and then explained why, Sebastiano was even more upset. He kept going, 'But I had your permish! I had your permish, Philippe!'

'My permission to use my daughter's image to promote your awful rags?' My father was disgusted. 'You most certainly did not!'

But Sebastiano kept insisting he had.

And little by little, it came out that he *had* had permission, in a way. Only not from me. And not my dad, either. Guess who, it appears, gave it to him?

Grandmere went, all indignantly, 'I only did it, Philippe, because Amelia, as you know, suffers from a terrible self-image and needed a boost.'

But my dad was so enraged he wouldn't even listen to her.

He just thundered, 'And so to repair her self-image you went behind her back and gave permission for her photos to be used in an advertisement for *women's clothing*?'

Grandmere didn't have much to say after that. She just stood there going, 'Uhn . . . uhn . . . uhn . . .' like someone in a horror movie who'd been pinned to a wall with a machete but wasn't quite dead yet (I always close my eyes during parts like this, so I know exactly what it sounds like).

It became clear that even if Grandmere had had a reasonable excuse for her behaviour, my father wasn't going to listen to it – or let me listen to it, either. He stalked over to me, grabbed my arm and marched me right out of the suite.

I thought we were going to have a bonding moment like fathers and daughters always do on TV, where he'd tell me that Grandmere was a very sick woman and that he was going to send her somewhere where she could take a nice long rest, but instead all he said was, 'Go home.'

Then he handed me over to Lars – after slamming the door to Grandmere's suite VERY loudly behind him – and stormed off in the direction of his own suite.

Jeez.

It just goes to show that even a royal family can be dysfunctional.

Couldn't you just see us on *Ricki Lake*?

Ricki: Clarisse, tell us: why did you allow Sebastiano to put your granddaughter's photos in that *Times* advertising supplement?

Grandmere: I did it to boost her self-esteem. And how dare you call me by my first name? That's Your Royal Highness to you, Ms Lake.

I just know that when I get to school on Monday, everybody is going to be all, 'Oh, look, here comes Mia, that big FAKE, with her vegetarianism and her animal-rights

144

activism and her looks-aren't-important-it's-what's-on-the-inside-that-matters-ism. But I guess it's all right to pose for *fashion photo shoots*, isn't it, Mia?'

As if it wasn't enough I had to be suspended. Now I am going to be sneered at by my peers too.

I'm home now, trying to pretend none of it ever happened. This is difficult, of course, because when I walked back into the loft I saw that my mom had already pulled the supplement out of our paper and drawn little devil horns coming out of my head in every picture, then stuck the whole thing on to the refrigerator.

While I appreciate this bit of whimsy, it does not make the fact that I will have to show my face – now plastered all over advertising supplements throughout the tri-state area – in school on Monday any easier.

Surprisingly, there is one good thing that's come out of all of this: I know for sure I look best in the white taffeta number with the blue sash. My dad says over his dead body am I going to wear it, or any other Sebastiano creation. But there isn't another designer in Genovia who could do as good a job – let alone finish the dress in time. So it looks like it's going to be the dress by Sebastiano, which got delivered to the loft this morning.

Which is one thing off my mind, anyway.

I guess.

Saturday, December 12, 8 p.m., the Loft

I have already gotten seventeen e-mails, six phone calls and one visitor (Lilly) about the fashion thing. Lilly says it's not as bad as I think and that most people throw the supplements away without even looking at them.

But if that's true, I said, why are all these people calling and e-mailing me?

She tried to make out like it was all members of the Students Against the Corporatization of Albert Einstein High School, calling to show their solidarity with my suspension, but I think we both know better:

It's all people who want to know what I was thinking, selling out like that.

How am I ever going to explain that I had nothing to do with it – that I didn't even *know* about it? Nobody is going to believe that. I mean, the proof is right there: I'm *wearing* the proof. There's photographic evidence of it.

My reputation is going down the drain, even as I sit here. Tomorrow morning, millions of subscribers to the *New York Times* are going to open their papers and be like, 'Oh, look, Princess Mia. Sold out already. Wonder how much she got paid? You wouldn't think she'd need the money, what with being royal and all.'

Finally I had to ask Lilly to please go home, because I'd developed such a headache. She tried to cure it with some shiatsu, which her parents frequently employ on their patients, but it didn't work. All that ended up happening was that I think she burst a blood vessel or something between my thumb and index finger, since it really hurts.

Now I am determined to start studying, even though it's Saturday night and everyone else my age is out having fun.

But haven't you heard? Princesses never get to have any fun.

Here is what I have to do:

- Algebra: review chapters 1–10
- English: term paper, 10 pages, double spaced, utilize appropriate margins; also, review chapters 1–7
- World Civ.: review chapters 1–12
- G & T: none
- French: revue chapitres Un–Neuf
- Biology: review chapters 1–12
- Write out instructions on how to care for Fat Louie.
- Christmas/Hanukkah shopping:
    Mom – Bon Jovi maternity T
    Dad – Book on anger management
    Mr G – Swiss Army knife
    Lilly – blank videotapes
    Tina Hakim Baba – copy of *Emanuelle*
    Kenny – combination TV/VCR (I don't think this is too extravagant. And no, it's not guilt, either. He really wants one)
    Grandmere – NOTHING!!!!!!
- Paint fingernails (maybe presence of foul-tasting polish will prevent biting them off)
- Break up with Kenny.
- Organize sock drawer.

I am going to start with the sock drawer because that is clearly the most important. You can't really concentrate on anything if your socks aren't right.

Then I will move on to Algebra because that is my worst subject, and also my first test. I am going to pass it if it is the last thing I do. NOTHING is going to distract me. Not this thing with Grandmere, not the fact that four of those seventeen e-mails are from Michael, not the fact that two are from

Kenny, not the fact that I am leaving for Europe at the end of next week, not the fact that my mother and Mr Gianini are in the next room watching *Die Hard*, my favourite Christmas movie, NOTHING.

I WILL PASS ALGEBRA THIS SEMESTER, and NOTHING IS GOING TO DISTRACT ME FROM STUDYING FOR THE FINAL!!!!!!!!!!!

Saturday, December 12, 9 p.m., the Loft

I just had to go out and see the part where Bruce Willis throws the explosives down the elevator shaft, but now I am back to work.

Saturday, December 12, 9:30 p.m., the Loft

I was really curious about what Michael could possibly
want, so I read his e-mails – just his. One was about the supplement (Lilly had told him, and he wanted to know if I was
thinking of abdicating, ha ha) and the other three were jokes
that I suppose were meant to make me feel better. They
weren't very funny but I laughed anyway.

I bet Judith Gershner doesn't laugh at Michael's jokes.
She's too busy cloning things.

How to Care for Fat Louie While I am Away:

a.m.

In the morning, please fill Fat Louie's bowl with **dry food**. Even if there is already food in the bowl, he likes to have some fresh served on top so he can feel like he is having breakfast like the rest of us.

In my bathroom is a **blue plastic cup** sitting by the bathtub. Please fill that every morning with water from the bathroom sink. You must use water from the **bathroom sink** because water from the kitchen sink isn't cold enough. And you have to put it in the **blue cup** because that is the cup Fat Louie is used to drinking out of while I am brushing my teeth.

He has a bowl in the hallway outside my room. Rinse that out and fill it with water from the **water filter pitcher** in the refrigerator. It must be water from the **water filter pitcher** because even though New York tap is said to be contaminant-free, it is good for Louie to get at least some water that is definitely pure. Cats need to drink a lot of water to flush out their systems and prevent kidney and urinary tract infections, so always leave lots of water out, and not just by his food bowls but other places as well.

Do not confuse the bowl in the hall with the **bowl by the Christmas tree**. That bowl is there to discourage Louie from drinking out of the tree holder. Too much tree resin could make him constipated.

In the morning, Fat Louie likes to sit on the window sill of my room and look at the pigeons on the fire escape. **NEVER OPEN THIS WINDOW**, but be sure the curtains are open so he can see out.

Also, sometimes he likes to look out the windows by the TV. If he cries while he is doing this, it means you should pet him.

p.m.

At dinnertime, give Fat Louie **canned food**. Fat Louie only likes three flavours, **Chicken and Tuna Feast (Flaked), Shrimp and Fish Feast (Flaked),** and **Ocean Fish Feast (Flaked)**. He won't eat anything with **beef** or **pork.** He must have the contents of the can on a new **CLEAN** saucer or he won't eat. Also, he won't eat if the contents don't retain their **can-like shape** on the plate, so don't chop up his food.

After eating his canned food, Fat Louie likes to stretch out on the carpet in front of the front door. This is a good time to give him his exercise. When he stretches out, just put your hand under his front legs and straighten them (he likes this) until he bends like a comma. Then dig your thumbs between his shoulder blades and give him a kitty massage. He will purr if you do it right. If you do it wrong you will know because he will bite you.

Fat Louie gets bored very easily and when he gets bored, he walks around crying, so here are some games he likes to play:

- Take some pieces of **cat treat** and line them up on top of the stereo for Fat Louie to knock off and chase.
- Put Fat Louie in my **computer chair** and then hide behind the bookshelf and throw one end of a shoelace over the back of the chair so he can't see where it is coming from.
- Make a **fort** out of pillows on my bed and put Fat Louie inside of it and then stick your hand into any openings between the pillows (I recommend wearing gloves during this game).
- Put some catnip in an **old sock** and throw it to Fat Louie. Then leave him alone for four to five hours, because catnip makes him a little free with his claws.

The Litter Box

Mr Gianini, this one is for you. Mom must not clean out the litter box or touch anything that may have come in contact with it or she might develop toxemia and she or the baby might die or get sick. Always wash your hands in warm, soapy water after changing Fat Louie's litter box, even if you don't think you got anything on your hands.

Fat Louie's box needs to be scooped out **every day**. Always use clumping litter and then just scoop out the clumps into a Grand Union bag and dispose. Nothing could be simpler. He tends to do number 2 about two hours after his evening meal. You will be able to tell from the odour wafting from his box in my bathroom.

Most Important of All

Remember not to disturb Fat Louie's **special area behind the toilet** in my bathroom. That is where he keeps his collection of shiny objects. If he takes something of yours and you find it there, be sure not to take it out while he is looking or for weeks he will try to bite you every time he sees you. I talked to the vet about it, but she said short of hiring an animal behaviourist at $70/hr there is nothing that can be done. We just have to put up with it.

Above all, be sure to pick Fat Louie up several times a day and hug and squeeze him!!!!! (He likes this.)

Saturday, December 12, Midnight, the Loft

I can't believe it's midnight already and I am still only on Chapter One of *An Introduction to Algebra*!

This book is incomprehensible. I sincerely hope whoever wrote it did not make very much money from it.

I should just go and ask Mr G what's going to be on the Final.

No, that would be cheating.

Wouldn't it?

Sunday, December 13, 10 a.m., the Loft

Only forty-eight hours until the Algebra final and I am still on Chapter One.

Sunday, December 13, 10:30 a.m., the Loft

Lilly just came over again. She wants to study for World Civ. together. I told her I can't worry about World Civ. when I am only on Chapter One in my Algebra review, but she said we could alternate: she would quiz me on Algebra for an hour – then I could quiz her on World Civ. for an hour. I said OK, even though it really isn't fair – she is getting an A in Algebra so her quizzing me isn't really helping her any, while my quizzing her in World Civ. helps me study for it too.

But that's what friends are for, I guess.

Sunday, December 13, 11 a.m., the Loft

Tina just called. Her little brothers and sisters are driving her crazy. She wanted to know if she could come down and study here. I said sure.

What else could I say? Besides, she promised to stop at H and H for bagels and vegetable cream cheese. And she said she thought the photos of me in the supplement were beautiful and that I shouldn't care if people call me a sellout because I look so hot.

Sunday, December 13, Noon, the Loft

Michael told Boris where Lilly was, so now Boris is here too.

Lilly's right. Boris really does breathe too loudly. It's very distracting.

And I wish he wouldn't put his feet on my bed. The least he could do is take his shoes off first. But when I suggested it, Lilly said that would be a bad idea.

Ew. I don't know why Lilly puts up with a boyfriend who is not only a mouth breather but also has stinky feet.

Boris may be a musical genius but he has a lot to learn about hygiene, if you ask me.

Sunday, December 13, 12:30 p.m., the Loft

Now Kenny's here. I don't know how I am supposed to get any studying done with all of these people around. Plus Mr Gianini has decided now would be a good time to practise his drums.

Sunday, December 13, 8 p.m., the Loft

I told Lilly and she agreed that once Boris and Kenny showed up, the whole studying thing kind of went down the drain. Plus Mr G's drumming didn't help. So we decided it would be best to take a study break and go to Chinatown for dim-sum.

We had a good time at Great Shanghai, eating vegetable dumplings and dried sautéed string beans with garlic sauce. I ended up sitting by Boris and he really made me laugh, engineering it so that whenever the waiters brought something new, the only empty spot on the table was in front of him so they had to put it there, which meant Boris and I got first dibs on it.

This made me realize that in spite of the sweaters and the mouth-breathing, Boris really is a funny and nice person. Lilly is so lucky. I mean, that the boy she loves actually loves her back. If only I could love Kenny the way Lilly loves Boris!

But I don't seem to have any control over who I fall in love with. Believe me, if I did I would NOT love Michael. I mean, for one thing he is my best friend's older brother, and if Lilly ever found out I liked him, she would NOT understand. Also, of course, he is a senior and is graduating soon.

And oh, yeah, he already has a girlfriend.

But what am I supposed to do? I can't *make* myself fall in love with Kenny, any more than I can *make* him stop liking me, you know, in that special way.

Although he still hasn't asked me to the dance. Or mentioned it at all. Lilly says I should just call him and be like, 'So are we going, or not?' After all, she keeps pointing out, I had the guts to smash up Lana's mobile. Why don't I have the guts to call my own boyfriend and ask him whether or not he is taking me to the school dance?

But I smashed up Lana's phone in the heat of passion. I cannot summon up anything like passion where Kenny is concerned. There is a part of me that doesn't want to go to the dance with him at all, and that part of me is relieved he hasn't mentioned anything about it.

OK, it is a very small part of me, but it is still *there*.

So actually, even though I was having fun sitting by Boris at the restaurant and all, it was also a little depressing, on account of the whole Kenny thing.

And then things got even more depressing. That's because some little Chinese-American girls came up to me as I was opening my fortune cookie and wanted to know if they could have my autograph. Then they handed me pens and the *advertising supplement* that had appeared in that day's *Times* for me to sign.

I seriously thought about killing myself, only I couldn't think how I'd do it, except for maybe stabbing myself through the heart with a chopstick.

Instead, I just signed the stupid thing for them and tried to smile. But inside, of course, I was FREAKING OUT, especially when I saw how happy the little girls were to have met me. And why? No, not because of my tireless work on behalf of the polar bears or the whales or starving kids. Which I haven't actually done yet, but I fully intend to do.

No, because I'd been in a magazine in a bunch of pretty dresses, and I'm tall and skinny like a model.

Which is no accomplishment at all!

After that, my headache came back and I said I had to go home.

Nobody protested very much – I think because everybody

162

realized all of a sudden how much time we'd wasted and how much studying we all had left to do. So we left, and now I am home again and my mom says that while I was gone Sebastiano called four times AND he had this dress delivered.

Not just any dress, either. It is a dress Sebastiano designed just for me. To wear to the Non-Denominational Winter Dance. It isn't sexy at all. It is dark green velvet with long sleeves and a wide square-shaped neckline.

But when I put it on and looked at my reflection in the mirror in my room, something funny happened:

I looked good. *Really* good.

There was a note attached to the dress that said:

> *Please forgive me.*
> *I promise this dress will not make him think of you*
> *as his little sister's best friend.*
>
> *S.*

Which is very sweet. Sad, but sweet. Sebastiano can't know, of course, that the Michael situation is completely hopeless and that no *dress* is going to make any difference, no matter how nice I look in it.

But, hey, at least Sebastiano *apologized*. That's a lot more, I've noticed, than Grandmere has done.

Of course I forgive Sebastiano. I mean, none of it his fault, really.

And I guess someday I'll probably forgive Grandmere since she's too old to know any better.

But the person I will never, ever forgive is myself for getting into this situation in the first place. I totally should have known better. I should have told Sebastiano 'No photos, please'.

Only I was so carried away, looking at myself in all those beautiful dresses, that I forgot being a princess is more than just wearing pretty dresses: it's being an example to a lot of people . . . people you don't even know and may not ever even meet.

Which is why if I don't pass this Algebra test, I am dead.

Monday, December 14, Homeroom

Here are the number of students at Albert Einstein High School who (so far) have felt compelled to make comments to me about my smashing Lana Weinberger's mobile phone last Friday:

37

Here are the number of students at Albert Einstein High School who (so far) have felt compelled to mention my suspension last Friday:

59

Here are the number of students at Albert Einstein High School who (so far) have felt compelled to make comments to me about my appearance in an advertising supplement to the *New York Times* over the weekend:

74

Total number of comments made to me so far today by students at Albert Einstein High School:

170

Oddly, after wading through all of this negativity, when I got to my locker I found something that seemed extremely out of place: a single yellow rose, sticking out of the door.

What can this mean? Can there be someone in this school who does not despise me?

Apparently so. But when I looked around, wondering who my one supporter could be, I saw only Justin Baxendale, being stalked (as usual) by a horde of worshipful girls.

I suppose my anonymous rose-leaver must be Kenny, trying to cheer me up. He will not admit it, but who else could it be?

It is Reading Day today, which means we are supposed to spend the whole day – except for lunch – sitting in

Homeroom, studying for Finals, which begin tomorrow. This is fine by me, since at least this way there's no chance I'll run into Lana. Her homeroom is on a whole other floor.

The only problem is that Kenny's in this class. We have to sit alphabetically, so he's way up at the front of this row, but he keeps passing notes back to me. Notes that say things like, *Keep on smilin'!* and *Hang in there, sunshine!*

He won't fess up to the rose thing, though.

By the way, want to know the total number of comments made to me so far today by Michael Moscovitz?

1

And it wasn't even really a comment. He told me in the hallway that my combat boot had come untied.

And it had.

My life is so over.

Five days until the Non-Denominational Winter Dance, and still no date.

Distance formula: d-10xrt
  r=10
  t=2
  d=10 + (10)(2)
  =10 + 20= 30

Variables are place holders for numbers (letters)

Distributive law
$5x + 5y - 5$
$5 (x + y - 1)$

$2a - 2b + 2c$
$2 (-1) - 2(-2) + 2 (5)$
$-2 + 4 + 10 = 12$

Four times a number is added to three, the result is five times the number.

Find the number.

x = the number
$4x + 3 = 5x$
$-4x \qquad -4x$
$3 = x$

Regardez les oiseaux stupides.

Cartesian coordinate system divides the plane into four parts called quadrants
  Quadrant 1 (positive, positive)
  Quadrant 2 (negative, positive)
  Quadrant 3 (negative, negative)
  Quadrant 4 (positive, negative)

Slope: slope of a line is line denoted m

Find slope
    negative slopes
    positive slopes
    zero slope

vertical line has no slope

horizontal line has 0 slope

    Collinear – points that lie on the same line

parallel lines have the same slope

$$4x + 2y = 6$$
$$2y = -4x + 6$$
$$y = -2x + 3$$

active voice indicates that the subject of the verb is acting
passive voice indicates that the subject of the verb is being
acted upon

Tuesday, December 15

Algebra and English finals completed.
Only three more, plus term paper, to go.

76 comments today, 53 of them negative:
'Sellout' = 29 times
I-Must-Think-I'm-All-That = 14 times
Here Comes Miss Thang = 6 times

Lilly says, 'Who cares what people are saying? You know the truth, right? And that's all that matters.'
That's easy for Lilly to say. Lilly's not the one who people are saying all those mean things about. *I* am.

Somebody left another yellow rose in my locker. What is up with that? I asked Kenny again if it was him, but he denied it. Strangely, he seemed to get very red in the face about it. But this might have been because Justin Baxendale, who was walking by at the time, stepped on Kenny's foot. Kenny has very large feet – larger even than mine.

Four more days until the Non-Denominational Winter Dance, and *nada* on the date front.

Wednesday, December 16

World Civ. exam *finis*.
   Two more, plus term paper, to go.

   62 comments, 34 negative:
   'Don't give up your day job' = 12 times
   'Sellout' = 5 times
   'If I was flat-chested like you, Mia, I could be a model too' = 6 times

1 rose, yellow, still no indication who left it. Perhaps someone is mistaking my locker for Lana's. She is, after all, always hanging out in that area, waiting for Josh Richter whose locker is next door to mine, so that the two of them can suck face. It is possible that someone thinks he is leaving roses for her.
   God knows, no one at Albert Einstein High School would want to leave flowers for me. Unless I were dead, maybe, and they could fling them on to my grave and say, 'Good riddance, Miss Thang.'

Three more days until the dance. Still nothing.

Thursday, December 17, 1 a.m.

It just occurred to me:

Maybe Kenny is lying about the roses. Maybe they really *are* from him. Maybe he's leaving them as kind of teasers, leading up to asking me to the dance tomorrow night.

Which is kind of insulting, really. I mean, him waiting this long to finally ask. For all he knows, I could have said yes to somebody else by now.

As if somebody else might have asked.
HA!

Thursday, December 17, 4 p.m., Limo on the Way to the Plaza

THAT'S IT!!!!!
  I'M DONE!!!!!!
  DONE WITH FINALS!!!!!!!!!!!!!
And guess what?

I'm pretty sure I passed all of them. Even Algebra. The grades aren't posted until tomorrow, during the Winter Carnival, but I bugged Mr G so much he finally said, 'Mia, you did fine. Now leave me alone, all right?'

Got that????? He said I did FINE!!!!!!!!!! You know what *fine* means, don't you?

IT MEANS I PASSED!!!!!!!!!!!!!!!!!

Thank God all of that's over. Now I can concentrate on what's important:

My social life.

I am serious. It is in a state of total disrepair. Everyone at school – with the exception of my friends – thinks I am this total sellout. They're like, 'You talk the talk, Mia, but you don't walk the walk.'

Well, I'm going to show them. Right after the World Civ. exam yesterday, it hit me like a ton of bricks. I knew *exactly* what to do. It's what Grandmere would do.

Well, OK, maybe not *quite* what Grandmere would do, but it will solve the whole problem. Granted, Sebastiano isn't going to like it very much. But, then, he should have asked ME, not Grandmere, if it was all right to run those photos in an ad for his clothes. Right?

I have to say, this is the most princessy thing I've done so far. And I am very, very nervous. Seriously. You wouldn't believe how much my palms are sweating.

But I cannot continue to lie back and meekly take this abuse. Something must be done about it, and I think I know what.

The best part is, I am doing it all by myself with no help from anyone.

Well, all right, the concierge at the Plaza helped by getting me a room, and Lars helped by making all the calls on his mobile phone.

And Lilly helped me write down what I was going to say, and Tina did my make-up and hair just now.

But other than that, it was all me.

OK, we're here.

Here goes nothing.

Thursday, December 17, 7 p.m.

I have now watched myself on all four major networks, plus New York 1, CNN, Headline News, MSNBC, and Fox News Channel. Apparently, they are also going to show it on *Entertainment Tonight*, *Access Hollywood* and *E! Entertainment News*.

I have to say, for a girl who supposedly has issues with her self-image, I think I did a fine job. I didn't mess up, not even once. And if I maybe spoke a little too fast, well, you could still *understand* me. Unless, you know, you're a non-English speaker or something.

I looked good too. I probably should have worn something other than my school uniform, but you know, royal blue comes off pretty good on TV.

The phone has been ringing off the hook ever since the press conference was first aired. The first time it rang, my mom picked it up and it was Sebastiano, screaming incomprehensibly about how I've ruined him.

Only he can't say ruined. It just came out 'rued'.

I felt really bad. I mean, I didn't mean to ruin him. Especially after he was so nice about designing me that dress for the dance.

But what was I supposed to do? I tried to make him look on the bright side:

'Sebastiano,' I said, when I got on the phone. 'I haven't ruined you. Really. It's just the proceeds from the sales of the dresses I'm wearing in the ad that will go to Greenpeace.'

But Sebastiano completely failed to look at the big picture. He kept screaming, 'Rued! I'm rued!'

I pointed out that far from ruining him, his donating all the proceeds from sales of the dresses I modelled to Greenpeace was going to be perceived in the industry as a

174

brilliant stroke of marketing genius, and that I wouldn't be surprised if those dresses flew off the racks since girls like me, who are really the people his fashions are geared for, care a great deal about the environment.

I must have picked up a thing or two during my princess lessons with Grandmere since in the end I totally won him over. By the time I hung up, I think Sebastiano almost believed the whole thing had been his idea in the first place.

The next time the phone rang it was my dad. I may have to scratch the plan to get him a book on anger management because he was laughing his head off. He wanted to know if it had been my mom's idea, and when I said, No, it was all me, he went, You really have got the princess thing down, you know.

So in a weird way I feel like I passed that Final too.

Except, of course, that I'm still not speaking to Grandmere. Not a single one of the calls I've gotten tonight (which even included Mamaw and Papaw back in Indiana, who saw the broadcast) have been from her.

Really, I think she should be the one to apologize because what she did was totally underhanded.

Almost as underhanded, my mom pointed out to me over dinner from Number One Noodle Son, as what I did.

Which is sort of shocking. I mean, I never thought about it before, but it's true: what I did tonight was as sneaky as anything Grandmere's ever done.

But I guess that shouldn't be very surprising. We are related, after all.

Then again, so were Luke Skywalker and Darth Vader.

Must go. *Baywatch* is on. This is the first time in weeks I've been home to watch it.

Thursday, December 17, 9 p.m.

Tina just called. She didn't want to talk about the press conference. She wanted to know what I got from my Secret Snowflake. I was all, 'Secret Snowflake? What are you talking about?'

'You know,' Tina said. 'Your Secret Snowflake. You remember, Mia. We signed up for it like a month ago. You put your name in the jar and then someone draws it, and they have to be your Secret Snowflake for the last week of school before Winter Break. They're supposed to surprise you with little gifts and stuff. You know, as a stress breaker. Since it's Finals week and all.'

I dimly remembered, one day before Thanksgiving Break, Tina dragging me over to a folding table where some nerdy-looking kids from the student government were sitting on one side of the cafeteria with a big jar filled with little pieces of paper. Tina had made me write my name on a slip of paper, then pick someone else's name out of the jar.

'Oh my God,' I cried. With all the stress of Finals and everything, I had forgotten all about it!

Worse, I had forgotten that I had drawn Tina's name. No real coincidence since she'd stuffed her slip of paper into the jar right before I picked. Still, what kind of heinous friend am I that I would forget something like this?

Then I realized something else. The yellow roses. They hadn't been put in my locker by mistake! And they really weren't from Kenny, either! They had to be from my Secret Snowflake.

Which was kind of upsetting in a way. I mean, it's really starting to look as if Kenny has no intention of asking me to tomorrow night's dance whatsoever.

'I can't believe you forgot about it,' Tina said, sounding

176

amused. 'You *have* been getting stuff for your Secret Snowflake, haven't you, Mia?'

I felt a rush of guilt. I had totally blown it. Poor Tina!

'Uh, sure,' I said, wondering where I was going to find a present for her by tomorrow morning, the last day of the Secret Snowflake thing. 'Sure, I have.'

Tina sighed. 'I guess nobody picked me,' she said. 'Because I haven't gotten anything.'

'Oh, don't worry,' I said, hoping the guilt washing over me wasn't noticeable in my voice. 'You will. Your Secret Snowflake is probably waiting, you know, until the last day because she's – or he's – gotten you something really good.'

'Do you think so?' Tina asked wistfully.

'Oh, yes,' I gushed.

Reassured, Tina got businesslike.

'Now,' she said, 'that Finals are over . . . '

'Um, yes?'

'. . . when are you going to tell Michael that you're the one who sent him those cards?'

Shocked, I went, 'How about never?'

To which Tina replied, tartly, 'Mia, if you don't tell him, then what was the point of sending those cards?'

'To let him know that there are other girls out there who might like him, besides Judith Gershner.'

Tina said severely, 'Mia, that's not enough. You've got to tell him it was you. How are you ever going to get him if he doesn't know how you feel?' Tina Hakim Baba, surprisingly, has a lot in common with my dad. 'Remember Kenny? That's how Kenny got you. He sent the anonymous notes but then he finally fessed up.'

'Yeah,' I said sarcastically. 'And look how great *that* turned out.'

'It'll be different with you and Michael,' Tina insisted.

'Because you two are destined for one another. I can just *feel* it. You've got to tell him, and it's got to be tomorrow, because the next day you are leaving for Genovia.'

Oh, God. In my self-congratulations over having successfully manoeuvered my first press conference, I'd forgotten about that too. I am leaving for Genovia the day after tomorrow! With Grandmere! To whom I am not even speaking any more!

I told Tina that I'd confess to Michael tomorrow and she hung up all happily.

But it was a good thing she hadn't been able to see my nostrils, because they were flaring like crazy on account of the fact that I was totally lying to her.

Because there is no way I am ever telling Michael Moscovitz how I feel about him. No matter what anyone says. I *can't*.

Not to his face.

Not ever.

Friday, December 18, Homeroom

They are holding us hostage here in Homeroom until they've passed out our final semester grades. Then we are free to spend the rest of the day at the Winter Carnival in the gym, and then, later this evening, the dance.

Really. We don't have any more classes after this. We are just supposed to have fun.

As if. I am so never having fun again.

That is because – aside from my many other problems – I think I know who my Secret Snowflake is.

Really, there is no other explanation. Why else would Justin Baxendale – who, even though he's so new is still totally popular, not to mention way good-looking – be hanging around my locker so much? I mean, seriously. This is the third time I've spotted him lurking around there this week. Why would he do that except to leave those roses?

Unless he's planning on blackmailing me about the whole fire alarm thing.

But Justin Baxendale doesn't exactly strike me as the blackmailer type. I mean, he looks to me like somebody who'd have something better to do than blackmail a princess.

Which leaves only one other explanation: he is my Secret Snowflake.

And how totally embarrassing is it going to be if I go out there when the bell rings, and Justin comes up to me to confess – because that's the rule, it turns out: you have to reveal your identity to your Secret Snowflake today – and I have to look up into his smoky eyes with those long lashes and give a big fake smile and go, 'Oh, gee, thanks, Justin. I had no idea it was you!'

Whatever. But actually, this is the least of my problems,

right? I mean, considering that I am the only girl in this entire school who does not have a date to the dance tonight. And that tomorrow I have to leave for a country I am princess of, with my lunatic grandmother who isn't speaking to my father, and who, I know from past experience, is not above smoking in the airplane lavatory, if the urge to do so strikes her.

Really. Grandmere is a flight attendant's worst nightmare.

But that's not even half of it. I mean, what about my mom and Mr Gianini? Sure, they are acting like they don't mind that I am going to be spending the holidays in another country. And, yes, we are going to have our own private little Christmas amongst ourselves before I leave. But really, I bet they mind. I bet they mind a lot.

And what about my grade in Algebra? Oh, Mr Gianini says it's fine, but what is fine, exactly? A D? A D is not fine. Not considering the number of hours I've put into raising my grade from an F, it isn't. A D is *not* acceptable.

And what – oh, God, *what* – am I going to do about Kenny?

At least I got Tina's present out of the way. I went on-line last night and signed her up for a teen romance book-of-the-month club. I printed out the certificate, saying she is an official member, and will give it to her when the bell rings.

Which is also when I have to go out there and face Justin Baxendale.

It wouldn't be so bad if it weren't for those eyes of his. Why does he have to be so good-looking? And why did someone like him have to pick me as his Secret Snowflake? Beautiful people, like Lana and Justin, can't help but be repulsed by ordinary-looking people like me.

He probably didn't even pull my name from that jar at all. Probably, he picked Lana's name and has been putting those roses in my locker, thinking it is Lana's, seeing as how God knows she never hangs out in front of her own locker.

What's even worse is that Tina told me yellow roses mean love *everlasting*.

Which of course was why I figured maybe Kenny was the one doing it after all.

Oh, great. They are passing around the printouts with our grades on them. I am not looking. I don't even care. I DO NOT CARE ABOUT MY GRADES.

Thank God for the bell. I'm just going to slip out of here – totally not looking at my grades – and go about my business like nothing out of the ordinary is going on.

Except, of course, when I get to my locker, Justin is there, looking for someone. Lana is there too, waiting for Josh.

You know, I really don't need this. Justin revealing that he is my Secret Snowflake right in front of Lana, I mean. God only knows what she's going to say – the girl who has been suggesting I wear Band Aids instead of a bra every day since the two of us hit puberty. Plus it isn't like she's been super-happy with me since the whole mobile phone thing. I'll bet she'll have something extra-mean all prepared for the occasion . . .

'Dude,' Justin says.

Dude? I am not a dude. Who is Justin talking to?

I turn around. Josh is standing there, behind Lana.

'Dude, I've been looking for you all week,' Justin says, to Josh. 'Do you have those Trig notes for me or not? I've got to make-up the Final in one hour.'

Josh says something, but I do not hear him. I do not hear him because there is a roaring sound in my ears. Because standing behind Justin is Michael.

Michael Moscovitz.

And in his hand is *a yellow rose.*

Friday, December 18, Winter Carnival

Oh, God.

I am in so much trouble.

Again.

And it isn't even my fault this time. I mean, I couldn't help myself. It just *happened*. And it doesn't mean anything. It was just, you know, one of those things.

Besides, it's not what Kenny thinks. Really. I mean, if you think about it, it is a complete and total letdown. For me, anyway.

Because, of course, the first thing Michael says when he sees me standing there gaping at him while he is holding that flower, is, 'Here. This just fell out of your locker.'

I took it from him in a complete daze. I swear to God my heart was beating so hard, I thought I was going to pass out.

Because I thought they'd been from him. The roses, I mean. For a minute there, I really did think Michael Moscovitz had been leaving me roses.

But of course this time, there's a note attached to the rose. It says:

Good luck with your trip to Genovia! See you when you get back!
Your Secret Snowflake,
Boris Pelkowski

Boris Pelkowski. Boris is the one who has been leaving those roses. Boris is my Secret Snowflake.

Of course, Boris wouldn't know that a yellow rose represents love everlasting. Boris doesn't even know not to tuck his sweater into his trousers. How would he know the secret language of flowers?

I don't know which was actually stronger, my feeling of relief that it wasn't Justin Baxendale leaving those roses after all . . .

. . . or my feeling of disappointment that it wasn't Michael.

Then Michael went, 'Well? What's the verdict?'.

To which I responded by staring at him blankly. I still hadn't quite gotten over it. You know, those brief few seconds when I'd thought – I'd actually thought, fool that I am – that he loved me.

'What did you get in Algebra?' he asked slowly, as if I were dense.

Which, of course, I am. So dense that I never realized how much in love with Michael Moscovitz I was until Judith Gershner came along and swept him right out from under my nose.

Anyway, I opened the computer printout containing my grades, and would you believe that I had raised my F in Algebra all the way up to a B minus?

Which just goes to show that if you spend nearly every waking moment in your life studying something, the likelihood is that you are going to retain at least a little of it.

Enough to get a B minus on the Final, anyway.

I'm trying really hard not to gloat, but it's difficult. I mean, I'm so happy.

Well, except for the whole not-having-a-date-to-the-dance thing.

Still, it's hard to be unhappy. There is absolutely no way I got this grade because the teacher happens to be my step-father. There's nothing subjective about Algebra, like in English. There's no interpretation of the facts. Either you're right or you're not.

And I was right. Eighty per cent of the time.

Of course, it helped that I knew the answer to the Final's extra credit question: What instrument did Ringo, in the Beatles, play?

But that was only worth two points.

Anyway, here's the part where I got into trouble. Even though, of course, it isn't my fault.

I was so happy about my B minus, I completely forgot for a minute how much I am in love with Michael. I even forgot, for a change, to be shy around him. Instead, I did something really unlike me.

I threw my arms around him.

Seriously. Threw my arms right around his neck and went, 'Wheeeeeee!!!!!'

I couldn't help it. I was so happy. OK, the whole rose thing had been a little bit of a bummer, but the B minus made up for it. Well, almost.

It was just an innocent hug. That's *all* it was. Michael had, after all, tutored me almost the whole semester. He had some stake in that B minus too.

But I guess Kenny, who Tina now tells me came around the corner right as I was doing it – hugging Michael, I mean – doesn't see it that way. According to Tina, Kenny thinks there's something going on between Michael and me.

To which, of course, I can only say, I WISH!

But I can't say that. I have to go find Kenny now and let him know, you know, it was just a friendly hug.

Tina's all, 'Why? Why don't you tell him the truth? That you don't feel the same way about him that he feels about you. This is your big chance!'

But you can't break up with someone during the Winter Carnival. I mean, really. How mean.

Why must my life be so fraught with trauma?

Friday, December 18, Still the Winter Carnival

Well, I still haven't found Kenny, but I really have to hand it to the administrators: grasping they might be, but they sure do know how to throw a party. Even Lilly is impressed.

Of course, signs of corporatization are everywhere: there are McDonald's orange drink dispensers on every floor, and it looks as if there was a run on Entenmann's, there are so many cake-and-cookie-laden tables scattered around.

Still, you can tell they are really trying to show us a good time. All of the clubs are offering activities and booths. There's ballroom dancing in the gym, courtesy of the Dance Club; fencing lessons in the auditorium, thanks to the Drama Club; even cheerleading lessons in the first-floor hallway, brought to us by, you guessed it, the junior varsity cheerleaders.

I couldn't find Kenny anywhere, but I ran into Lilly at the Students for Amnesty International booth (Students Against the Corporatization of Albert Einstein High School did not submit their application for a booth in time to get one, so Lilly is stuck running the Amnesty International booth instead). And guess what? Guess who got an F in something?

That's right.

'Lilly.' I couldn't believe it. 'Mrs Spears gave you an F in English? *YOU* got an F?'

She doesn't seem too bothered by it, though.

'I had to take a stand, Mia,' she said. 'And sometimes, when you believe in something, you have to make sacrifices.'

'Sure,' I said. 'But an *F*? Your parents are going to kill you.'

'No, they won't,' Lilly said. 'They'll just try to psycho-analyse me.'

Which is true.

Oh, God. Here comes Tina.

I hope she doesn't remember—

She does.

We're going over to the Computer Club's booth right now.

I don't want to go to the Computer Club's booth. I already looked over there, and I know what's going on. Michael and Judith and the rest of the computer nerds are sitting behind all these colour monitors. When somebody comes up, they get to sit down in front of one of monitors and play a computer game the club designed where you walk through the school and all of the teachers are in funny costumes. Like Principal Gupta is wearing a leather dominatrix's outfit and holding a whip, and Mr Gianini is in footie pyjamas with a teddy bear that looks exactly like him.

They used a different program when the club applied to be part of the carnival, of course, so none of the teachers or administrators know what everyone is sitting there looking at. You would think they'd wonder why all of the kids are laughing so hard.

Whatever. I don't want to do it. I don't want to go anywhere near it.

But Tina says I have to.

'Now's the perfect time to tell him,' she says. 'I mean, Kenny's nowhere to be seen.'

Oh, God. This is what comes from telling your friends anything.

Even Later on Friday, December 18,
Still the Winter Carnival

Well, I'm in the Girls' Room again. And I think I can state with certainty that this time I'm never coming out.

I'm just going to stay in here until everyone has gone home. Only then will it be safe. Thank God I am leaving the country tomorrow. Maybe by the time I get back, everyone involved in this little incident will have forgotten about it.

But I doubt it. Not with my luck, anyway.

Why do these kinds of things always happen to me? I mean, seriously? What did I ever do to turn the gods against me? Why can't they pick on Lana Weinberger? Why always *me*?

All right, so here's what happened.

I had no intention whatsoever of actually telling Michael anything. I mean, let me get that out right away. I was only going along with Tina because, well, it would have looked weird if I had completely avoided the Computer Club's booth. Plus Michael had asked me so many times to make sure I stopped by. So there was no way I could avoid it.

But I never intended to say a word about You-Know-What. I mean, Tina was just going to have to learn to live with disappointment. You don't love somebody for like as long as I have loved Michael, and then just go up to him at a school fair and be like, 'Oh, by the way, yeah, I love you.'

OK? You don't *do* that.

But whatever. So I went up to the stupid booth with Tina. Everyone was all giggly and excited because their program was so popular there was this really long line. But Michael saw us and went, 'Come on up!'

Like we were supposed to cut in front of all these other people. I mean, we did it, of course, but everyone behind us grumbled, and who can blame them? They'd been waiting a long time.

But I guess because of the thing the night before – you know, when I explained on national television that the only reason I'd done that clothing ad was because the designer was donating all the proceeds to Greenpeace – I have been noticeably more popular (positive comments so far: 243. Negative: 1. From Lana, of course). So the grumbling wasn't as bad as it could have been.

Anyway, Michael was all, 'Here, Mia, sit at this one.' And he pulled out a chair in front of this one monitor.

So I sat down and waited for the stupid thing to come on, and all around me other kids were laughing at what they were seeing on their screens. I just sat there thinking, for some reason, *Faint heart never won fair lady.*

Which was stupid because, number one, I was NOT going to tell him I like him and, number two, Michael is dark-haired, *not* fair. And he isn't a lady either, obviously.

Then I heard Judith go, 'Wait, what are you doing?'

And then I heard Michael say, 'No, that's OK. I have a special one for her.'

Then the screen in front of my eyes flickered. I sighed. OK, I thought. Here goes the stupid teacher thing. Be sure to laugh so they think you like it.

I was sitting there, and I was actually kind of depressed because I really didn't have anything to look forward to, if you think about it. I mean, everybody else was all excited because later on they were going to the dance, but no one had asked me to the dance – not even my supposed boyfriend – so I didn't even have that to look forward to. And everyone else I knew was going skiing or to the Bahamas or wherever for Winter Break, and what did I get to do? Oh, hang out with a bunch of members of the

Genovian Olive Growers Association. I'm sure they are all really nice people, but come on.

But before I even leave for my boring trip to Genovia, I have to break up with Kenny – something I totally don't want to do because I really do like him and I don't want to hurt his feelings, but I guess I sort of have to.

Although I have to say, the fact that he still hasn't so much as mentioned the dance is making the idea of breaking up with him seem a lot less heinous.

Then tomorrow, I thought, I'll leave for Europe on a plane with my dad and Grandmere, who still aren't speaking to one another (and since I'm not speaking to Grandmere either, it should be a really fun flight), and when I come back, knowing my luck, Michael and Judith will be engaged.

That's what I was sitting there thinking in the split second the screen in front of me flickered. That, and *You know, I'm not really in the mood to see any of my teachers in funny outfits.*

Only when the flickering stopped, that's not what I saw. What I saw instead was this castle.

Seriously. It was a castle, like out of the knights of the Round Table, or Beauty and the Beast, or whatever. And then the picture zoomed in until we were over the castle walls and inside this courtyard, where there was a garden. In the garden, all these big fat red roses were blooming. Some of the roses had lost their petals, and you could see them lying on the courtyard floor. It was really, really pretty, and I was like, *Hey, this is cooler than I thought it would be.*

And I sort of forgot I was sitting there in front of a computer monitor at the Winter Carnival, with like two dozen people all around me. I began to feel like I was actually *in* that garden.

Then this banner waved across the screen, in front of the

roses, like it was blowing in the wind. The banner had some words written on it in gold leaf. When it stopped flapping, I could read what the words said:

Roses are red
Violets are blue
You may not know it
But I love you too

I screamed and jumped up out of my chair, tipping it over behind me.

Everyone started laughing. I guess they thought I'd seen Principal Gupta in her leather catsuit.

Only Michael knew I hadn't.

And Michael wasn't laughing.

Only I couldn't look at Michael. I couldn't look anywhere, really, except at my own feet. Because I couldn't believe what had just happened. I mean, I couldn't process it. What did it *mean*? Did it mean Michael knew I was the one who'd been sending him those notes and that he felt the same way?

Or did it mean he knew I was the one who'd been sending him those notes, and he was trying to get back at me as a kind of joke?

I didn't know. All I knew was that if I didn't get out of there, I was going to start crying . . .

. . . and in front of everyone in the entire school.

I grabbed Tina by the arm and yanked her, *hard*, after me. I guess I was figuring I could tell her what I'd seen, and maybe *she'd* know what it meant, since I sure didn't.

Tina shrieked – I must have grabbed her harder than I thought – and I heard Michael call, 'Mia!'

But I just kept going, lugging Tina behind me, and pushing through the crowd for the door, thinking only one thing:

190

Must get to the Girls' Room. Must get to the Girls' Room before I start bawling my head off.

Somebody, with about as much force as I'd grabbed Tina, grabbed me. I thought it was Michael. I knew if I so much as looked at him, I'd burst into big baby sobs. I said, 'Get *off*,' and jerked my arm away.

It was Kenny's voice that said, 'But, Mia, I *have* to talk to you!'

'Not *now*, Kenny,' Tina said.

But Kenny was totally inflexible. He went, 'Yes, *now*,' and you could tell from his face he meant it.

Tina rolled her eyes and backed off. I stood there, my back to the Computer Club's booth, and prayed, *Please, please don't come over here, Michael. Please stay where you are. Please, please,* PLEASE *don't come over here.*

'Mia,' Kenny said. He looked more uncomfortable than I'd ever seen him, and I've seen Kenny look plenty uncomfortable. He's an awkward kind of guy. 'I just want to . . . I mean, I just want you to know. Well. That I know.'

I stared at him. I had no idea what he was talking about. Seriously. I'd forgotten all about that hug he'd seen in the hallway. The one I'd given Michael. All I could think was, *Please don't come over here, Michael. Please don't come over here, Michael . . .*

'Look, Kenny,' I said. I don't even know how I got my tongue to work, I swear. I felt like a robot somebody had switched into the Off position. 'This really isn't a good time. Maybe we could talk later—'

'Mia,' Kenny said. He had a funny look on his face. 'I *know*. I saw him.'

I blinked.

And then I remembered. Michael, and the B minus hug.

'Oh, Kenny,' I said. 'Really. That was just . . . I mean, there's nothing—'

'You don't have to worry,' Kenny said. And then I realized why his face looked so funny. It was because he was wearing an expression on it that I had never seen before. At least, not on Kenny. The expression was resignation. 'I won't tell Lilly.'

Lilly! Oh, God! The last person in the world I wanted to know how I felt about Michael!

Maybe it wasn't too late. Maybe there was still a chance I could . . .

But no. No, I couldn't lie to him. For once in my life, I could not summon up a lie.

'Kenny,' I said. 'I am so, so sorry.'

I didn't realize until I said it that it was too late to run for the Girls' Room: I had already started crying. My voice broke, and when I put my hands to my face, they came away wet.

Great. I was crying, and in front of the entire student body of Albert Einstein High School.

'Kenny,' I said, sniffling. 'I honestly meant to tell you. And I really do like you. I just don't . . . love you.'

Kenny's face was very white, but he didn't start crying – not like me. Thank God. In fact, he even managed to smile a little in that weird, resigned way as he said, shaking his head, 'Wow. I can't believe it. I mean, when it first hit me, I was like *no way*. Not Mia. No way would she do that to her best friend. But . . . well, I guess it explains a lot. About, um, us.'

I couldn't look him in the face any longer. I felt like a worm. Worse than a worm, because worms are very environmentally helpful. I felt like . . . like . . .

Like a fruit fly.

'I guess I've suspected for a long time that there was someone else,' Kenny went on. 'You never . . . well, you never exactly seemed to return my ardour when we . . . you know.'

I knew. Kissed. Nice of him to bring it up, though, here in the gym, in front of everyone.

'I knew you just weren't saying anything because you didn't want to hurt my feelings,' Kenny said. 'That's the kind of girl you are. And that's why I put off asking you to the dance because I figured you'd just say no. On account of you, you know, liking someone else. I mean, I know you'd never lie to me, Mia. You're the most honest person I've ever met.'

HA! Was he joking? *Me*? Honest? Obviously, he did not have the slightest clue about my nostrils.

'That's how I know that this must be tearing you up inside. I just think you better tell Lilly soon,' Kenny said sombrely. 'I started to suspect, you know, at the restaurant. And if I figured it out, other people will too. And you wouldn't want her to hear it from somebody else.'

I had reached up to try to wipe some of my tears away with my sleeve, but paused with my hand only halfway there, and stared at him. 'Restaurant? What restaurant?'

'You know,' Kenny said, looking uncomfortable. 'That day we all went to Chinatown. You and he sat next to each other. You kept laughing . . . you looked pretty chummy.'

Chinatown? But Michael hadn't gone with us that day to Chinatown . . .

'And you know,' Kenny said, 'I'm not the only one who's noticed him leaving you those roses all week, either.'

I blinked. I could barely see him through my tears. 'W-what?'

'You know.' He looked around, then dropped his voice to a whisper. 'Boris. Leaving you all those roses. I mean, come on, Mia. If you two want to carry on behind Lilly's back, that's one thing, but—'

The roaring in my ears that had been there just after I'd read Michael's poem came back.

BORIS. BORIS PELKOWSKI. My boyfriend just broke up with me because he thinks I am having an affair with **BORIS PELKOWSKI**.

BORIS PELKOWSKI, who always has food in his braces.

BORIS PELKOWSKI, who wears his sweaters tucked inside his trousers.

BORIS PELKOWSKI, my best friend's boyfriend.

Oh, God. My life is so over.

I tried to tell him. You know – the truth. That Boris isn't my secret love, but my Secret Snowflake.

But Tina darted forward, grabbed me by the arm and went, 'Sorry, Kenny, Mia has to go now.' Then she dragged me into the Girls' Room.

'I have to tell him,' I kept saying over and over like a crazy person, as I tried to break free of her grip. 'I have to tell him. I have to tell him the truth.'

'No, you do not,' Tina said, pushing me past the toilet stalls. 'You two are broken up. Who cares why? You're through, and that's all that matters.'

I blinked at my tear-stained reflection in the mirror above the sinks. I looked awful. Never in your life have you seen anyone who looked less like a princess than I did then. Just looking at myself made me break out into a fresh wave of tears.

Of course Tina says she's sure Michael wasn't trying to make fun of me. Of course she says that he must have figured out that I was the one who was sending him those cards, and was trying to let me know that he feels the same way about me.

Only of course I can't believe that. Because if that were true – *if that were true* – why did he let me go? Why didn't he try to stop me?

194

Tina has pointed out that he did try. But my shrieking when I read his poem, and then running in tears from the room, might not have seemed to him like a very encouraging sign. In fact, it might have actually looked to him like I was displeased by what I'd seen. Furthermore, Tina pointed out, even if Michael had tried to go after me, there'd have been Kenny cornering me on my way out. It had certainly looked as if the two of us were Having A Moment – which we most certainly were – and didn't wish to be disturbed.

All of which could be true.

But it could also be true that Michael was just joking. A very mean joke under the circumstances, but Michael doesn't know that I love him with every fibre of my being. Michael doesn't know that I've been in love with him all my life. Michael doesn't know that without him, I will never, ever achieve self-actualization. I mean, to Michael, I'm just his kid sister's best friend. He probably didn't mean to be cruel. He probably thought he was being funny.

It isn't his fault that my life is over and that I am never, ever leaving this bathroom.

I'll just wait until everybody is gone, and then I'll sneak out, and no one will see me again until next semester starts, by which time, hopefully, all of this will have blown over.

Or, better yet, maybe I'll just stay in Genovia . . .

Hey, yeah. Why not?

Friday, December 18, 5 p.m., the Loft

I don't know why people can't just leave me alone.

Seriously. I may be done with Finals, but I still have a lot to do. I mean, I have to pack, don't I? Don't people know that when you are leaving for your royal introduction to the people over whom you will one day reign, you have to do a lot of packing?

But no. No, people keep on calling, and e-mailing, and coming over.

Well, I'm not talking to anybody. I think I have made that perfectly clear. I am not speaking to Lilly, or Tina, or my dad, or Mr Gianini, or my mother, and ESPECIALLY not Michael, even though at last count he'd called four times.

I am *way* too busy to talk to anybody.

And with my headphones on, I can't even hear them pounding on the door. It's kind of nice, I have to say.

Friday, December 18, 5:30 p.m., the Fire Escape

People have a right to their privacy. If I want to go into my room and lock the door and not come out or have to deal with anyone, I should have a right to. People should *not* be allowed to take the hinges off my door and *remove* it. That is completely unfair.

But I have found a way to foil them. I am out on the fire escape. It is about thirty degrees out here and, by the way, it's snowing. But guess what? So far no one has followed me.

Fortunately, I bought one of those pens that is also a flashlight, so I can see to write. The sun went down a while ago, and I have to admit my butt is freezing. But it's actually sort of nice out here. All you can hear is the hiss of the snow as it lands on the metal of the fire escape, and the occasional siren or car alarm. It is restful, in a way.

And you know what I'm finding out? I need a rest. Bigtime.

Really. I need to like go and lie on a beach somewhere or something.

There's a nice beach in Genovia. With white sand, palm trees, the whole bit.

Too bad while I'm there, I'm never going to have time to visit it, since I'm going to be too busy christening battle ships or whatever.

But if I *lived* in Genovia . . . you know, moved there and lived there full time . . .

Oh, I'll miss my mom, of course. I've already considered that. She's leaned out the window about twenty times already, begging me to come inside, or to at least put on a coat. My mom's a nice lady. I'll really miss her.

But she can come visit me in Genovia. At least, up until her eighth month. Then air travel might be a little risky. But she can come after my baby brother or sister is born. That would be nice.

And Mr G, he's OK too. He just leaned out and asked if I wanted any of the four alarm chilli he just made. He left out the meat, he says, just for me.

That was nice of him. He can come visit me in Genovia too.

It will be nice to live there. I can hang out with my dad all the time. He's not such a bad guy, either, once you get to know him. He wants me to come in off the fire escape too. I guess my mom must have called him. He says he's really proud of me, on account of the press conference and my B minus in Algebra and all. He wants to take me out to dinner to celebrate. We can go to the Zen Palatte, he says. A totally vegetarian restaurant. Isn't that nice of him?

Too bad he let Lars take my door down or I might have gone with him.

Ronnie, our next-door neighbour, just looked out her window and saw me. Now she wants to know what I'm doing, sitting out on the fire escape in December.

I told her I needed some privacy, and that this appears to be the only way I can get it.

Ronnie went, 'Honey, don't I know how that is.'

She said I was going to freeze without a coat though, and offered me her mink. I politely declined as I cannot wear the skins of dead animals.

So she loaned me her electric blanket, which she has plugged into the outlet beneath her air conditioner. I must say, this is an improvement.

Ronnie is getting ready to go out. It is nice to watch her put on her make-up. As she does it, she is keeping up a running conversation with me through the open window. She asked me if I was having trouble at school and if that was why I'm on the fire escape, and I said I was. She asked what kind and I told her. I told her I am being persecuted: that I am in love with my best friend's brother, but that to him it is apparently all this really big joke. Oh, and also that everyone apparently thinks I am having an affair with a mouth-breathing violinist who happens to be my best friend's boyfriend.

Ronnie shook her head and said it was good to know things haven't changed since she was in high school. She says she knows what it is like to be persecuted, because Ronnie used to be a man.

I told Ronnie that it really doesn't matter, because I'm moving to Genovia. Ronnie said she was sorry to hear that. She'll miss me, as I have really improved conditions in the apartment building's incinerator room since I insisted on installing separate recycling bins for newspapers and cans and bottles.

Then Ronnie said she has to go because she's meeting her boyfriend for cocktails at the Carlyle. She said I could keep the electric blanket, though, so long as I remember to put it away when I'm done using it.

God. Even my next-door neighbour, who used to be a man, has a boyfriend. WHAT IS WRONG WITH ME????

Uh-oh. I hear footsteps in my room. Who's coming now?

Friday, December 18, 7:30 p.m.

Well. You could knock me over with a feather.

Guess who just came out onto the fire escape and sat with me for half an hour?

Grandmere.

I am not even kidding.

I was sitting here, feeling all depressed, when all of a sudden this big furry sleeve appeared out my window, and then a foot in a high-heeled shoe, and then a big blonde head, and next thing I knew, Grandmere was sitting there, blinking at me from the depths of her full-length chinchilla.

'Amelia,' she said, in her most no-nonsense tone. 'What are you doing out here? It's snowing. Come back inside.'

I was shocked. Shocked that Grandmere would even consider coming out on to the fire escape (it is an indelicate thing for a princess to mention, but there is actually a lot of bird poop out here), but also that she would dare to speak to me, after what she did.

But she addressed that issue right away.

'I understand that you are upset with me,' she said. 'And you have a right to be. But I want you to know that what I did, I did for you.'

'Oh, right!' Even though I swore I was never going to speak to her again, I couldn't help myself. 'Grandmere, how can you possibly say that? You completely humiliated me!'

'I didn't mean to,' Grandmere said. 'I meant to show you that you are just as pretty as those girls in the magazines you are always wishing you looked like. It's important that you know that you are not this hideous creature that you apparently think you are.'

'Grandmere,' I said. 'That's nice of you and all – I guess – but you shouldn't have done it that way.'

200

'What other way could I do it?' Grandmere demanded. 'You will not pose for any of the magazines that have offered to send photographers. Not for *Vogue*, or *Harper's Bazaar*. Don't you understand that what Sebastiano said about your bone structure is true? You really are quite beautiful, Amelia. If only you'd just have a little more confidence in yourself – show off once in a while. Think how quickly that boy you like would leave the house fly girl for you!'

'Fruit fly,' I said automatically. 'And, Grandmere, I told you, Michael likes her because she's really smart. They have a lot of stuff in common – like computers. It has nothing to do with how she looks.'

'Oh, Mia,' Grandmere said. 'Don't be naive.'

Poor Grandmere. It really wasn't fair to blame her, because she comes from such a different world. In Grandmere's world, women are valued for being great beauties – or, if they aren't great beauties, they are revered for dressing impeccably. What they do, like for a living, isn't important, because most of them don't do anything. Oh, maybe they do some charity work, or whatever, but that's it.

Grandmere doesn't understand, of course, that today being a great beauty doesn't count for much. Oh, it matters in Hollywood, of course, and on the runways in Milan. But nowadays, people understand that perfect looks are the result of DNA – something the person has nothing to do with. It's not like it's any great accomplishment, being beautiful. It's just genetics.

No, what matters today is what you do with the brain *behind* those perfect blue eyes (or brown eyes, or green, or whatever). In Grandmere's day, a girl like Judith, who could clone fruit flies, would be viewed as a piteous freak unless she managed to clone fruit flies *and* look stunning in Dior.

Even in this remarkably enlightened age, girls like Judith

201

still don't get as much attention as girls like Lana – which isn't fair, since cloning fruit flies is probably way more important than having totally perfect hair.

The really pathetic people are the ones like me: I can't clone fruit flies *and* I've got bad hair.

But that's OK. I'm used to it by now.

Grandmere's the one who still needs convincing that I am an absolutely hopeless case.

'Look,' I said to Grandmere. 'I told you. Michael is not the type of guy who is going to be impressed because I'm in a *Sunday Times* supplement in a strapless ballgown. *That's why I like him.* If he were the kind of guy who was impressed by stuff like that, I wouldn't want anything to do with him.'

Grandmere didn't look very convinced.

'Well,' she said. 'Perhaps you and I must agree to disagree. In any case, Amelia, I came over to apologize. I never meant to distress you. I meant only to show you what you can do, if you'd only try.' She spread her gloved hands apart. 'And look how well I succeeded. Why, you planned and executed an entire press conference, all on your own!'

I couldn't help smiling a little at that one. 'Yes,' I said. 'I did.'

'And,' Grandmere said, 'I understand that you passed Algebra.'

I grinned harder. 'Yes. I did.'

'Now,' Grandmere said, 'there is only one thing left for you to do.'

I nodded. 'I know. And I've been thinking a lot about it. I think it might be best if I extended my stay in Genovia. Like maybe I could just live there from now on. What do you think about that?'

Grandmere's expression, I could see in the light coming from my room, was one of disbelief.

'Live in . . . live in Genovia?' For once, I'd caught her off guard. 'What are you talking about?'

'You know,' I said. 'I could just finish ninth grade in school there. And then maybe I could go to one of those Swiss boarding schools you're always going on about.'

Grandmere just stared at me. 'You'd hate it.'

'No,' I said. 'It might be fun. No boys, right? That would be great. I mean, I'm kind of sick of boys right now.'

Grandmere shook her head. 'But your friends . . . your mother . . . '

'Well,' I said reasonably. 'They could come and visit.'

Then Grandmere's face hardened. She peered at me from between the heavily mascaraed slits her eyelids had become.

'Amelia Mignonette Grimaldi Renaldo,' she said. 'You are running away from something, aren't you?'

I shook my head innocently. 'Oh, no, Grandmere,' I said. 'Really. I'd like to live in Genovia. It'd be neat.'

'NEAT?' Grandmere stood up. Her high heels went through the slots between the metal bars of the fire escape, but she didn't notice. She pointed imperiously at my window.

'You get inside right now,' she hissed, in a voice I had never heard her use before.

I have to admit, I was so startled I did exactly what she said. I unplugged Ronnie's electric blanket and crawled right back into my room. Then I stood there while Grandmere crawled back in too.

'You,' she said, when she'd straightened out her skirt, 'are a princess of the royal house of Renaldo. A princess,' she said, going to my wardrobe, and rifling through it, 'does not shirk her responsibilities. Nor does she run at the first sign of adversity.'

'Um, Grandmere,' I said. 'What happened today was hardly the first sign of adversity, OK? What happened today was the last straw. I can't take it any more, Grandmere. I am getting out.'

Grandmere pulled from my wardrobe the dress Sebastiano had designed for me to wear to the dance. You know, the one that was supposed to make Michael forget that I am his little sister's best friend.

'Nonsense,' Grandmere said.

That was all.

Just 'nonsense'. Then she stood there, tapping her toes and staring at me.

'Grandmere,' I said. Maybe it was all that time I'd spent outside. Or maybe it was that I was pretty sure my mom and Mr G and my dad were all in the next room, listening. How could they not be? There was no *door*, or anything, to separate my room from the living room.

'You don't understand,' I said. 'I can't go back there.'

'All the more reason,' Grandmere said, 'for you to go.'

'No,' I said. 'First of all, I don't even have a date for the dance, OK? And P.S., only losers go to dances without dates.'

'You are not a loser, Amelia,' Grandmere said. 'You are a princess. And princesses do not run away when things become difficult. They throw their shoulders back and they face what disaster awaits them head on. Bravely, and without complaint.'

I said, 'Hello, we are not talking about marauding Visi-goths, OK, Grandmere? We are talking about an entire high school that now thinks I am in love with Boris Pelkowski.'

'Which is precisely,' Grandmere said, 'why you must show them that it doesn't matter to you what they think.'

204

'Why can't I show them that it doesn't matter by not going?'

'Because that,' Grandmere said, 'is the cowardly way. And you, Mia, as you have shown amply this past week, are not a coward. Now get dressed.'

I don't know why I did what she said. Maybe it was because somewhere deep inside, I knew that for once, Grandmere was right.

Or maybe it was because secretly, I guess I was a little curious to see what would happen.

But I think the real reason was because, for the first time in my entire life, Grandmere didn't call me Amelia.

No. She called me Mia.

And because of my stupid sentimentalism, I am in a car right now, going back to stupid crappy Albert Einstein High School, the dust from which I thought I'd managed to shake permanently from my feet not four hours ago.

But no. Oh, no. I'm going back, in the stupid velvet party dress Sebastiano designed for me. I'm going back and I will probably be ridiculed for being the dateless biological freak that I am.

But regardless of what happens, I can always comfort myself with the knowledge of one thing:

Tomorrow, I will be thousands of miles away from all of this.

Oh, God. We're here.

I think I'm going to be sick.

Saturday, December 19, Royal Genovian Jet

When I was about to turn six years old, all I wanted for my birthday was a cat.

I didn't care what kind of cat. I just wanted one – a cat of my very own. We had been to visit my mom's parents at their farm in Indiana, and they had a lot of cats. One of them had had kittens – little fluffy orange and white ones, which purred loudly when I held them under my chin, and liked to curl up inside the bib of my overalls and nap. More than anything in the world, I wanted to keep one of those kittens.

I should mention that, at the time, I had a thumb-sucking problem. My mother had tried everything to get me to stop sucking my thumb, including buying me a Barbie, in spite of her fundamental stand against Barbie and all that she stands for, as a sort of bribe. Nothing worked.

So when I started whining to her about wanting a kitten, my mom came up with a plan. She told me she would get me a kitten for my birthday if I quit sucking my thumb.

Which I did, immediately. I wanted a cat of my own *that badly.*

And yet, as my birthday rolled around, I had my doubts my mother would live up to her end of the bargain. For one thing, even at the age of six I knew my mom wasn't the most responsible person. Why else was our electricity always being turned off? And about half the time I showed up at school wearing a skirt AND trousers, because my mother let *me* decide what I wanted to wear. So I wasn't sure she'd remember about the kitten – or that, if she did remember, she'd know where to get one.

So as you can imagine, when the morning of my sixth birthday rolled around, I wasn't holding out much hope.

But when my mother came into my bedroom holding this tiny ball of yellow and white fur and plopped it on to my chest, and I looked into Louie's (he didn't become Fat Louie until about twenty-something pounds later) great big blue eyes (this was before they turned green), I knew a joy such as I had never known before in my life and never expected to feel again.

That is, until last night.

I am totally serious.

Last night was the best night of my ENTIRE life. After that whole fiasco with Sebastiano and the photos, I thought I would never ever feel anything like gratitude to Grandmere EVER again.

But she was SO RIGHT to make me go to that dance. I am SO GLAD I went back to Albert Einstein, the best, the loveliest school, in the whole country, if not the whole world!!!!!!!

OK, here's what happened:

Lars and I pulled up in front of the school. There were twinkly white lights in all the windows that I guess were supposed to represent icicles or whatever.

I was sure I was going to throw up and I mentioned this to Lars. He said I couldn't possibly throw up because to his certain knowledge I hadn't eaten anything since the Entemann's cake way before lunch, and that was probably all digested by now. With that piece of encouraging information, he escorted me up the steps and into the school.

There were masses of people teeming around the coat check in the front entrance. Lars checked our coats while I stood there waiting for someone to come up and ask me what I was doing there without a date. All that happened, however, was that Lilly-and-Boris and Tina-and-Dave descended upon me, and started acting all nice and said how happy they were that I'd come (Tina told me later that she'd already explained to everyone that Kenny and I had broken up, although she hadn't told them why, THANK GOD).

So, fortified by my friends, I went into the gym, which was decorated all wintery with cut-out paper snowflakes, one of those disco balls, and fake snow everywhere, which I must say looked a lot whiter and cleaner than the snow that was starting to pile up on the ground outside.

There were tons of people there. I saw Lana and Josh (ugh), Justin Baxendale with his usual flock of adoring fans, and Shameeka and Ling Su and a bunch of other people. Even Kenny was there, though when he saw me he went bright red and turned around and started talking to this girl from our Bio. class. Oh well.

Everyone was there, except the one person I'd been most dreading. Or hoping to see. I didn't know which.

Then I saw Judith Gershner. She had changed out of her overalls and looked quite pretty in this red Laura Ashleyish dress.

But she wasn't dancing with Michael. She was dancing with some boy I'd never seen before.

So I looked around for Lilly and finally spotted her using one of the payphones. I went up to her and was like, 'Where's your brother?'

Lilly hung up the phone. 'How should I know?' she demanded. 'It's not my turn to babysit him.'

I went – oddly comforted by her demeanour, which simply proved that no matter how much other things change, Lilly always stayed the same – 'Well, Judith Gershner is here, so I just figured—'

'For God's sake,' Lilly said. 'How many times do I have to tell you? *Michael and Judith are not going out.*'

I went, 'Oh, right. Then why have they spent every waking moment together for the past two weeks?'

'Because they were working on that stupid computer program for the Carnival,' she said. 'Besides, Judith Gershner already has a boyfriend.' Lilly grabbed me by the shoulders and turned me around so I could see Judith on the dance floor. 'He goes to Trinity.'

I looked at Judith Gershner as she slow-danced with a boy who looked a lot like Kenny, only older and not as uncoordinated.

'Oh,' I said.

'Oh is right,' Lilly said. 'I don't know what is wrong with you today, but I can't deal with you when you're acting like such a freak. Sit down right here' – she pulled out a chair – 'and don't you dare get up. I want to know where to find you when I need to.'

I didn't even ask Lilly why she might need to find me. I just sat down. I felt like I couldn't stand up any more. I was *that* tired.

It wasn't that I was disappointed. I mean, I didn't want to see Michael. At least, part of me didn't.

Another part of me *really* wanted to see him and ask him just what he'd meant by that poem.

But I was sort of afraid of the answer.

Because it might not be the one I was hoping it would be.

After a while, Lars and Wahim came and sat down next to me. I felt like a complete tool. I mean, there I was, sitting at a dance with two bodyguards, who were deep in a discussion about the advantages versus the disadvantages of rubber bullets. Nobody was asking me to dance. Nobody would, either.

Why was I even staying? I had done what Grandmere said. I had shown up. I had proved to everyone that I wasn't a coward. Why couldn't I leave? I mean, if I wanted to?

I stood up. I said to Lars, 'Come on. We've been here long enough. I still have a lot of packing to do. Let's go.'

Lars said OK and started to get up. Then he stopped. I saw that he was looking at something behind me. I turned around.

And there was Michael.

He had obviously just gotten there. He was out of breath. His bow tie wasn't tied and there was still snow in his hair.

'I didn't think you were coming,' he said.

I knew my face had gone as red as Judith Gershner's dress. But there wasn't anything I could do about that. I said, 'Well, I almost didn't.'

He said, 'I called you a bunch of times. Only you wouldn't come to the phone.'

I said, 'I know.' I was wishing the floor of the gym would open up, like in *It's a Wonderful Life*, and that I'd fall into the pool underneath it and drown and not have to have this conversation.

'Mia,' he said. 'With that thing today. I didn't mean to make you cry.'

Or the floor could open and I could just fall and keep falling, for ever and ever and ever. That would be OK too. I stared at the floor, willing it to crack apart and swallow me up.

'It didn't,' I said. 'I mean, it wasn't that. It was something Kenny said.'

'Yeah,' Michael said. 'Well, I heard you two broke up.'

Yeah. Probably by now the whole school had. Now, I knew, my face was even redder than Judith's dress.

'The thing is,' Michael went on, 'I knew it was you. Who was leaving those cards.'

If he had reached inside my chest, pulled out my heart, flung it to the floor and kicked it across the room, it could not possibly have hurt as much as hearing that. I could feel my eyes filling up with tears all over again.

'You did?' You know, it's one thing to have your heart broken. But to have it happen at a school dance, in front of everyone . . . well, that's harsh.

'Of course I did,' he said. He sounded impatient. 'Lilly told me.'

For the first time, I looked up into his face.

'*Lilly* told you?' I cried. 'How did *she* know?'

He waved his hand. 'I don't know. Your friend Tina told her, I guess. But that's not important.'

I looked around the gym and saw Lilly and Tina at the far side of it, both staring in my direction. When they saw me looking at them, they turned around really fast and pretended to be deeply absorbed in conversation with their dates.

'I'm going to kill them,' I murmured.

Michael reached out and grabbed both my shoulders. 'Mia,' he said, giving me a little shake. 'It doesn't *matter*. What matters is that I meant what I wrote. And I thought you did too.'

I didn't think I could have heard him right. I went, 'Of course *I* meant it.'

He shook his head. 'Then why did you freak out like that today at the carnival?'

I stammered, 'Well, because . . . because . . . I thought . . . I thought you were making fun of me.'

'Never,' he said.

And that's when he did it.

No fuss. No asking my permission. No hesitation whatsoever. He just leaned down and kissed me, right on the lips.

And I found out, right then, that Tina was right:

It *isn't* gross if you're in love with the guy.

In fact, it's the nicest thing in the whole world.

And do you know what the best part is?

I mean, aside from Michael being in love with me, and having kept it a secret almost as long as I have, if not longer?

And Lilly knowing all along but not saying anything up until a few days ago because she found it an interesting social experiment to see how long it would take us to figure it out on our own (a long time, it turned out)?

And the fact that Michael's going to Columbia next year, which is only a few subway stops away so I'll still be able to see him as much as I want?

Oh, and Lana walking by while we were kissing, and going, in this disgusted voice, 'Oh, God, get a room, would you?'

And slow dancing with him all night long, until Lilly finally came up and said, 'Come on, you guys, it's snowing so hard, if we don't leave now we'll never get home'?

And kissing good night outside the stoop to my loft, with the snow falling all around us (and grumpy Lars complaining he was getting cold)?

No, the best part is that we moved right into Frenching without any trouble at all. Tina was right – it just seemed perfectly natural.

And now the captain says we have to put away our tray tables for take-off, so I'll have to quit writing in a minute.

Dad says if I don't stop talking about Michael, he's going to go sit up front with the pilot for the flight.

Grandmere says she can't get over the change in me. She says I seem taller. And you know, maybe I am. She thinks it's because I'm wearing another one of Sebastiano's original creations, designed just for me, just like the dress that was supposed to make Michael see me as more than just his

212

little sister's best friend . . . except that it turned out he already did. But I know that's not it.

And it isn't love, either. Well, not entirely.

I'll tell you what it is: self-actualization.

That and the fact that it turns out I'm really a princess, after all. I must be, because guess what?

I'm living happily ever after.

The
PRINCESS
DIARIES
Princess Club

HEY, PRINCESS,
WANNA JOIN THE PRINCESS DIARIES PRINCESS CLUB?

4 fantastic comps and regular doses of fashion, gossip and games direct 2 ur mobile txt ur date of birth (dd,mm,yy)

to **07950 080700**

You will also get FREE unpublished snippets, exclusive games & comps!

08,11,91

The
PRINCESS
DIARIES

Mia Goes Fourth

Princess Mia Thermopolis's Royal Resolutions:

- I will stop biting my fingernails.

- I will be kinder to everyone, even cheerleaders.

- I will spend every waking moment thinking about Michael Moscovitz!

Mia's back from her first royal trip to Genovia.
Now she's ready for what's REALLY important: her love life.

Mia and Michael are finally an item, but Grandmere seems to have other plans. Just before the happy couple's first hot date, an unmissable royal engagement turns up. Could it be that Michael doesn't measure up – and that (please not!) Grandmere's got someone else in mind for Princess Amelia Mignonette Grimaldi Thermopolis Renaldo?

Look out for GIVE ME FIVE – the fifth part of Mia's hilarious diaries. She's the most unlikely princess – ever!